THE WOONBOOT

Woody Starkweather

THE WOONBOOT

Table of Contents

MAP OF THE NETHERLANDS

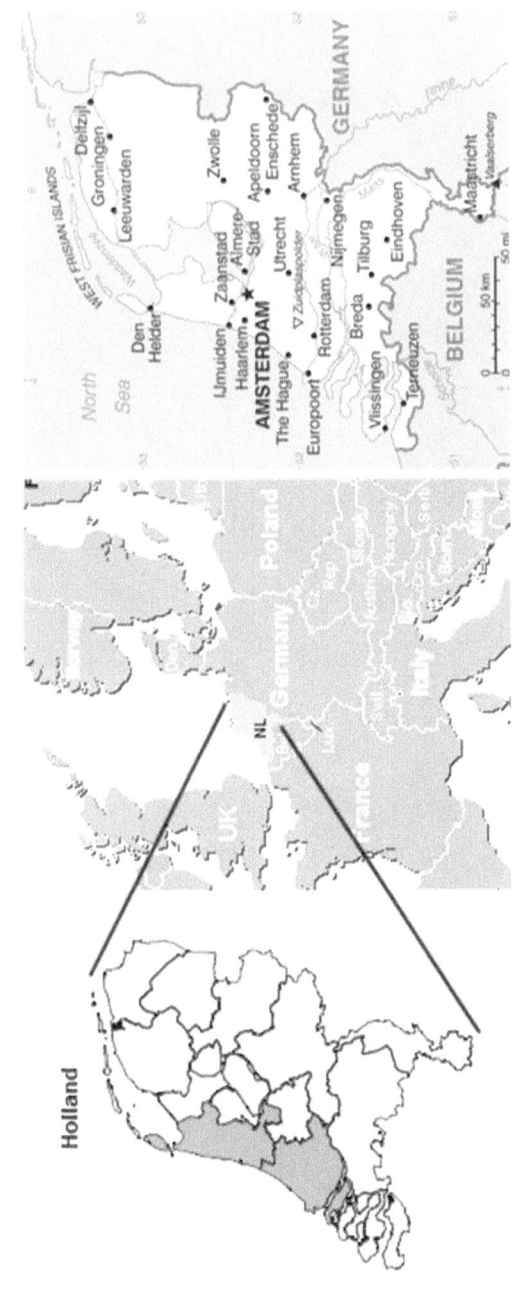

Chapter 1
The Beginning

They had less than a minute. The Saudis always followed the same routine and Louise had timed them. Charles popped the trunk open. Louise felt around in the grocery bags. It was already getting dark at four in the afternoon in Amsterdam, and the trunk light was dim. Her hand found a melon. Quickly, she sank the hypodermic into the melon and pressed the plunger. It went down slowly, too slowly. She didn't know how much of the contaminated water had gotten in, but it would have to do. She took the needle out, and with her other hand she felt around some more.

"One minute to go," Charles said, looking at his watch. "You'll have to hurry." He shook his head. "They call themselves terrorists, but they don't know enough to lock their trunk."

"Or vary their routine," added Louise.

She groped around in another bag. Something soft, wrapped in paper. Meat, she thought, and she plunged the needle in deep and injected the rest of the syringe.

"OK. That should keep them busy," she said as she withdrew the needle.

"Happy New Year," Charles said.

He lowered the trunk lid and pressed it down until it clicked, engaging the latch with as little noise as possible. Louise dumped the hypodermic into her pocketbook.

They both straightened up and walked away, forcing themselves to walk slowly, and listening behind them. If they'd been cats, their ears would have turned around. They heard the hatch of the woonboot open, right on schedule, and the Saudi's light footsteps on the deck, then crossing the other woonboot, and stepping on to the quay. They kept walking slowly. They were about five car lengths away when they heard him lift the trunk, then the crinkle of paper as he gathered the shopping bags into his arms, a slam as he shut the trunk, probably with his elbow they guessed, and then the footsteps again back on the decks.

He set the bags down with a crunching sound while he lifted the woonboot hatch, then he called out in Arabic.

Charles recognized it—a call for someone to help him with the packages. An answering sound came fainter, from inside, and then another voice in the winter air. Soon after that the hatch closed again.

Charles reached over and took Louise's hand, slipping his index finger in between her little and ring finger in their special way of holding hands. They were clear now. They both let their breath out at the same time.

"We're OK," Charles said.

"But they are in for a very bad night," said Louise.

"Yes they are," Charles agreed. "By the way, I've got another idea, but I'll need some computer assistance."

"What are you going to do?" she asked.

"I'm going to play God," said Charles.

Back in their little apartment across the street, down a few houses and up one flight, they listened to the bug Charles had planted earlier. They heard the rustling of brown paper bags and the dull clanking of canned goods being placed on shelving, as the men in the woonboot put away their groceries. In a few hours there'd be a lot of moaning.

Charles looked out the window. He could make out the woonboot, lit by a streetlamp across the canal. It lay still in the ice-covered water. He chuckled a little, thinking that it might start rocking at about 2:00 AM. There was only one toilet for the six of them. But from a distance and at night it looked quite peaceful. It made him think about their home in Virginia. It

8

would be warmer there, no ice on their little canal, and the sky might be clear. There might be snow geese flying at night, honking quietly in the gloom as if whispering. Here in Amsterdam the sky was always cloudy in January.

***

A month earlier, Charles and Louise had received another call from the President's Office, sending them out on a new mission far too soon after they had returned from Costa Rica, where they had tracked down a war criminal who had escaped from the International Court in Belgium. They'd been looking forward to some relief from the heart-thumping close calls and near misses of that operation by spending time in their quiet house by the water.

They lived on a small island off the Virginia Eastern Shore divided from the mainland by tidal waters and channels and bridged by a long causeway. Whenever they returned home from one of their missions, the view from the causeway welcomed them. On sunny days, everything was in shades of rich brown and deep blue and flashing white. The marsh grasses varied from wheaten beige to straw blonde, and the water could be a brilliant dark sapphire blue in the salt ponds or the somber gray of deeper water. The blue and brown scene was dotted in white by gulls, terns, egrets, and plovers and a dozen species of ducks, all plying their particular trade—wheeling and driving, wading and striking, swimming, paddling, dabbling, taking off and landing. There was in fact so much constant motion from swooping and soaring in snowy white, sooty gray, and iridescent green, that it was dazzling to come upon, and it was easy to overlook the small, still patches of crimson flowers surrounded by the beige grass, offset by the deep blue pools of tidal water.

Charles liked to roll the window down and smell deeply. He could identify exactly, with his remarkable nose, many of the plants and animals of the inland waterways, and he'd taken the trouble to mentally catalogue the different smells associated with the tidal stages, so that with one whiff and a little thought, he knew quite a lot about the state of things on the water.

For Louise, the first sight of their house, nestled in among the loblolly pines at the end of the road, helped her feel that she was fully back into normal reality. The log house was on the sea side of the island, but on a shallow bay separating the island from a barrier island, which protected them from the Atlantic Ocean itself. She was always delighted when they came upon the house, small and rustic, settled firmly on the land next to the water. It was their world, comfortable and safe.

On this return, she walked around the house and saw that it was in good shape. A small snowfall earlier in the week had left a thin covering on the grass. Her feet pressed the snow down, revealing the grass in partial footprints that were oddly shaped—a heel in one place that looked like an iron kettle, a toe in another place shaped like a Tyrolean hat—green hieroglyphics against a white background. It would all be gone in two hours as the sun warmed up the ground and the salt air.

The forsythia buds were closed up tight for the winter. An ornamental cherry tree—a gift when they first bought the house—found no hint of warmth in the air, and the few minutes of more sunshine each day meant that spring was approaching but still not near. The cherry buds were still tightly closed against the possibility of frost, but looking very closely, Louise saw that now, in February, some swelling was discernible; in less than a month blossoms would burst out.

The outside walls of the log house had been treated with water repellent the summer before and still looked shiny and clean. They'd repaired some damage done by insects during the past summer, and those repairs too were holding. She walked around the house to the water side.

She found Charles looking out at the bay, where the sunlight flashed off wavelets stirred by a growing breeze. Two boats moved along in the channel between the two islands. They were too far away to hear their motors. Probably duck hunters, surely the first of the season, returning home after an early morning shoot. They would veer out of the channel soon and head across the shallows to a house, where a hearty breakfast and fresh hot coffee would warm them for the task of cleaning their kill in the weak morning sun.

In the little inlet that bordered their property and gave them access to the deeper water, they saw a male grebe, not more than 30 feet away, his orange topknot brilliant in the sunlight, performing figure eights in the calm water. They'd never seen it before, but it had to be a mating signal. Why else would he swim compulsively in repeated figure eights? It seemed unlikely that any birds would be mating in the late fall. They watched, feeling a little sorry for the horny grebe. No sweetly drab girl grebe flew down to join him. Maybe there weren't any in these parts, and the male's signals were a wasted effort. They reminded Charles of himself when he was young, standing on a street corner with his friends watching girls go by. They too had hoped that by putting themselves out in the open, a passing female would get the idea and come gliding in on soft wings to make conversation. Maybe the grebe's figure eights were not perfect enough, and come to think of it, maybe Charles' admiring looks at passing girls had not been exactly what captivated a teenage heart. Certainly the result was the same— frustration, fatigue, and then resignation. They could almost hear the grebe muttering "Oh, forget it" to himself as he flew away.

Back inside, they turned on the systems, and Charles lit the fire he'd carefully laid in the Franklin stove. It caught easily enough, but there was an early burst of smoke that backed down the chimney for a few minutes before a good draw was established, and then, after the fire was well lit, there was an odd odor, which Charles identified immediately as an animal that had died trapped in the chimney. They heard a soft thump as its body, shrunk and dried by the smoke and fire, lost its purchase on the bricks and tumbled down to the elbow where the stovepipe came into the house. Since the fire seemed now to be drawing well, they concluded that the body was very small -- a sparrow or a mouse -- and that by now it was thoroughly desiccated. They hovered around the stove for a while, until the fire had warmed the place up. Then they brought in their bags and unpacked. The climbing sun poured both light and heat in through the kitchen windows.

As soon as the local stores were open, they went shopping for the essentials—groceries for the first home meals they would eat, after a mixed diet of foreign dishes, followed by airline food which was, in its own way, even more foreign.

They picked up things from the drug store and checked at the Post Office, where a package of letters, bills, and a huge blob of second-class advertisements and catalogs was handed to them. They waved to their next-door and across-the-street neighbors when they saw them, and visited with some of their close friends. Charles and Louise used the same cover story -- that they went on assignments as journalists for a magazine read by retirees -- but telling these lies to people they liked bothered them. They had to remind themselves of the higher purpose of their work. Within a couple of days, they were back in the retired couple routine.

Louise flew to Columbus to visit her young grandchildren, and Charles called his nieces and nephews. His two grandchildren were close enough for a day's visit, and he called to arrange for it. While Louise was gone, Charles looked at some woodworking projects he had begun many months earlier. He hauled the small sailboat he was building down from the garage rafters and examined it. The coat of paint he'd applied too hastily before he left was still crazed and wrinkled. He knew it would be, and he'd already planned to remove it right down to the wood and begin again under better conditions. He considered going fishing or duck-hunting, but when he compared rising early and going out on the water in a wet boat on a cold morning to sitting by a warm stove fire with a good book, the book and fire kept winning the argument.

***

Louise was still away when Henderson called on Charles' cell phone. Charles was in his shop, examining again the boat he'd almost finished building. The President wanted to see them. Charles felt protest rising in his mind. It was so soon after the last assignment. Usually, they had a month or two before they were asked to deal with something new.

Charles sighed after he hung up the phone.

"Too soon," he muttered to himself. He put his tools away before calling Louise, who had to cut her visit in Columbus a little short to catch the next flight to Baltimore. She packed quickly and kissed everyone goodbye, then took a cab to the airport. She didn't have long to wait at the airport and was lucky to get in at ten o'clock that same morning. Charles drove to the airport to pick her up.

He liked meeting her in an airport, and from the smile she gave him at the gate, so did she. They kissed and hugged each other warmly and then walked, arms around each other's waists, toward the parking lot. Charles carried her small suitcase. He asked her how the grandchildren were doing, and of course they were fine. She asked him if he knew anything about the President's summons, but of course he didn't. In the car, they were both quiet, wondering what might lie ahead. Louise loved the adventure of what they did; Charles enjoyed the sense of accomplishment but could do with a little less adventure.

Charles and Louise showed their passes at the White House gate, parked in an area reserved for very special guests, and picked up an escort inside the building who whisked them along toward the Oval Office. They asked for a bathroom break along the way—it had been a long drive in heavy traffic, and they had to pee and spruce up a little. The intern waited silently in the hall, tapping her foot as if she barely tolerated the delay. The contrast between elemental bathroom activities and the loftiness of the surroundings tickled Charles' sense of humor. The intern was young and impressed with herself. She wouldn't have seen the humor.

These talks with the President were nerve-wracking too. The assignment itself was usually dangerous, and the meetings with the President were important enough to jangle nerves. Always conscious of their citizenship and honored to serve their country in their own special way, they made sure not to waste the President's time. Like teenagers before a big date, they wanted everything to be perfect.

Chapter 2
The Assignment

They greeted Mrs. Skolnick, the President's secretary, warmly and got back the cold formality she was famous for. She made them wait a bit, as always—a ritual with her to make sure they felt the full weight of the President's importance. After a few minutes, she announced their names to the President and told them to go in.

Henderson was already there, with handshakes all around and congratulations on the success of their last mission. There were no jokes. Time was precious.

President Borden was, from their perspective, a young man. A southerner whose charm and good looks fit seamlessly with his forthright speaking style. These personal traits and his carefully centrist political stance had made him impossible to beat. The campaign had been hard fought and close at the end, which seemed to have become the norm. Charles and Louise were delighted at Borden's win. They'd worked for other presidents before him, but they liked him enormously, and he had a way of expressing his appreciation for their work that made them always willing and often eager to take on an assignment.

"Well, we meet again," he said with a smile. "I have to tell you (his Southern accent always made him seem like an old friend) I'm glad we're meetin' again. There were too many close calls the last time."

"Thank you for your concern, Mr. President," said Louise. "We're happy about the way it turned out too."

"OK. Here's what's goin' on. I want you two to go to the Netherlands. There are several cells of known terrorists operatin' there. We know about 'em. The Dutch know about 'em. In some cases, the terrorists even know that we know about 'em. But there are some that don't know we're on to them, and it's one of these that I want y'all to get involved with. We actually have a man inside this cell so we know what they're doin.' But our guy can't do much to stop them without lettin' on to them that he's a mole. Of course, given certain developments, such as an imminent attack, he'd do that, but for everything else his hands are tied."

The President's southern drawl disappeared as he got more serious about the assignment. Charles and Louise had seen it happen before.

He went on. "The Dutch police won't do anything until the terrorists break a law, which they haven't. You know the Dutch—very respectful of personal liberties. So, what we want you folks to do is make their lives difficult, slow them down, make it hard for them to buy food, talk on the phone, go from one place to the other—harass them in every way you can. Hell, let the air out of their tires. Slow down their whole operation, and it might make them desperate or frustrated enough to make a mistake. But don't get caught. We were asked by the Dutch government to do this, so we will not disavow you, but getting caught would lead to something in the press, and that could be embarrassing for us. Henderson of course will give you all the details. Do you have any questions?"

"Do we know what they're trying to do?" Charles asked.

"Yes, we do. We know a great deal. Henderson can brief you."

They took this second mention of Henderson as a signal that the interview was over, and they stood up. More handshakes, and they left. They went with Henderson to a small nearby office, where an aide was just putting down the phone. Young, blonde, and with her blue eyes veiled behind studious looking glasses, she had the same look that so many Presidential aides had—smart, ambitious, and a little cold. She must have been told to vacate her premises for a few minutes—she hurried out the door, giving them a sheepish smile.

They all sat down. Henderson opened a red notebook and began to give them details. There were six men in the cell, living together in a "woonboot." He pronounced it the way it was spelled so that the first syllable rhymed with "moon." The correct pronunciation was more like "voneboat," but Charles didn't bother to correct him. A woonboot—*living boat* in Dutch—was a river barge that had been converted into living quarters. It was not the same as a "huisboot", which meant the same thing as "houseboat" in English. This woonboot was tied to a quay on a canal in an area outside Amsterdam. The woonboot could be moved if necessary—it had its own power—but that was not the idea. These boats stayed put, and their addresses were registered with the Post Office. They might as well have been sitting on a foundation in the ground.

Of the six men, four were Saudis, one was a Kuwaiti, and one was an American. Charles and Louise were disappointed to learn that it was the Kuwaiti, not the American, who was the mole. But when they thought about it, it would be a little too obvious to have an American mole in an Arabic cell.

The Saudis were three brothers and a cousin. They were full of righteous anger and had left Saudi Arabia for Pakistan, eager to fight the Americans. They stayed in Pakistan for training, but the training hadn't been very good—not what it used to be. They were trained in handling small weapons, and there was lots of physical exercise. The training in how to assemble, place, and detonate explosives was more intensive; these were the skills they would need for their assigned mission.

After training, they'd been sent on to the Netherlands, along with three other cells. Although they had trained with the other three cells, once on site they were not supposed to meet. Each cell was as independent as possible. In some cases, the cell never had any contact with the leaders at all, until the day came when they got a signal to attack. Money was deposited in an account to keep the cells housed and fed.

The fledgling terrorists had been disappointed not to have an American target, but they told themselves that the Dutch government was just a puppet of the American infidels, something the Dutch would have found faintly amusing. Their target was the World Court at The Hague. When they were given the signal, they would assemble a bomb and set it off in one of the Court's meeting rooms.

Although they had already learned how to make the bomb, and how to set it off, they did not actually construct it. For that, the Dutch authorities could have them all arrested. But they knew where all the parts were located. They could get the components in a few hours, and assemble the bomb in five minutes. The assembly was left until the last minute to ensure that they wouldn't be caught and arrested. Timing was important, so they had to practice, and they'd been told that they would get a signal to go through a practice run, just to see if they could manage the timing of gathering the bomb components together, assembling the bomb and detonating it at the right location.

They'd been to The Hague several times, taken tours, studied maps, learned where all the important people had their offices and where they parked their cars. They were ready, living in the woonboot, waiting for a signal.

***

Charles and Louise flew directly to Schiphol Airport. The Dutch authorities had asked for their help, so they were welcome in the country and could bring their sophisticated computer equipment through customs without difficulty. On this mission they were not spies, just specialists.

They took a train to the center of the city and checked into a hotel. They would not stay long at the hotel; they needed to live near the woonboot to be effective. But they liked to spend a day or two getting used to the time change.

After checking in, they went to their room and slept for a few hours. Conventional wisdom said that travelers should stay awake and outdoors during daylight hours to get rid of jet lag, but they always found this advice very difficult to follow. Instead, they tried to change their sleep cycle as early as possible, sleeping on the plane, even though it was impossible to get a real night's rest.

When they got up, they felt better. It was then lunchtime, and they had a typical Dutch lunch of *boterhammen*—small meat and cheese sandwiches, mostly bread. They took a train out to the area where the woonboot was. The train let them off a few blocks from their destination, and they walked slowly along the canal. They had memorized the address. Louise, with her orientation skills, knew exactly where they were.

As they walked along the sidewalk, parallel to the canal, they could see that every inch of dock space was taken up by woonboots of many different kinds, often tied up double, so that an outer woonboot was tied to an inner one that was tied to the dock. In typical Dutch fashion, most of the woonboots had lace curtains in the tiny windows and containers for flowers hanging outside the windows, although nothing bloomed in the December chill. There was something faintly ridiculous about treating the little eyebrow windows of a woonboot as if it were a normal sized window in the living room of an ordinary house, but for the Dutch, window treatment was an important cultural heritage. In the old days, when religion was the dominant force in the Netherlands, the village priests would walk around the neighborhood, looking in people's windows to make sure that there was no sin taking place in the house. The people, eager to demonstrate their innocence, always left the windows unshuttered so that the priest could see in. The curtains they hung were designed not to hide the interior of the house from external view but to invite those outside to look in. Even in modern times, the Dutch paid close attention to their windows and the pulled back curtains that framed them.

The American couple consulted their memories as they walked along and found the woonboot they were interested in without difficulty.

"There it is," said Louise, pointing. "It's bigger than I thought it would be."

It was large, black all over, and a complete boat, not just a barge. It had a modest superstructure holding a wheelhouse, and had been self-propelled in its day.

"I wonder if it can still run," said Charles. "With proper care, the engine should work."

It was moored on the outside of another woonboot, similar in size but a dark red color.

"It must be inconvenient, and annoying, for the people living on an inside boat," said Louise, "to have people tramping overhead to get to the outside boat. Maybe they pay some money for the right to moor on the outside and cross over. A little money can reduce annoyance."

After they got a look at the woonboot, which was quiet enough for them to conclude that no one was home, they looked around at the neighborhood. A street ran alongside the dock, with a row of connected houses on the side away from the canal. These too were decorated with lace curtains and flowerboxes, and the houses were connected to one another just like the old stately houses along the main canals of Amsterdam, although these were newer and much wider. They looked like housing for the moderately wealthy. Above the roofs, a low cloud cover scudded along, and on the street the wind was chilling and intrusive. The houses looked like refuges of warmth and hospitality against the winter weather. The woonboots tried, but did not quite achieve, the same aura of coziness. Inside, they may have been as comfortable and friendly as any interior, but from the outside it was not easy to imagine beckoning hospitality in these squat, rounded, dark barges with the tiny eyebrow windows, surrounded by the iced over surface of a narrow canal. They were, in fact, somewhat forbidding, despite the lace curtains.

"We may have to disturb the complacency of this charming area," said Charles.

"It is peaceful, isn't it?" Louise said. "It would be a nice place to live for someone who worked in Amsterdam. It's near the train station and only fifteen minutes to the main part of the city."

"The ice must be thin," Charles said.

"What makes you think so?"

"There are no skaters." A second thought crossed his mind. "I wonder if the ice ever gets thick enough to damage those old wooden hulls. Probably not, or there wouldn't be so many of them." And there were many. Looking down the canal, he could see that the quay was lined with woonboots of many colors and different sizes. Obviously, housing in Amsterdam was at a premium, as it was throughout the densely-populated country.

They found a small restaurant, on the corner across from the train station, where they could sit in warmth and plan their activities over good Dutch coffee, the traditional symbol of Dutch hospitality, accompanied by a few cookies. The host was a genial man with a round red face and a very bald head who recognized them immediately as Americans and gestured to them that they could sit anywhere they liked. The gesture wasn't really necessary. They spent so much time in Europe and Asia that they were used to finding a table on their own.

"Well, the obvious thing is the woonboot," Charles began, leaning forward on his elbows on the table, still feeling a little heavy-lidded from lack of sleep.

"It is vulnerable, isn't it," Louise mused. She seemed to be contemplating the sinking of the woonboot with the kind of detachment a person might have about the thought of going to a ball game or the art museum.

Charles shook his head slowly. "Of course, we could sink it, but that would force them to move, and then we would have to start all over again. It has to be something less dramatic—a slow leak perhaps. That would get them scrambling, and they wouldn't have time to do much else until they got it fixed. I'm remembering that our mission is to slow them down."

"OK. That's one idea. What else?" Louise was always eager to get started, and she really relished the idea of making the lives of a few terrorists miserable. Later, after she had gotten to know them a little, she might soften her cutthroat attitude but for the moment it felt good to contemplate playing a devilish role. They were impish gnomes who would show terrorists that it didn't pay to adopt irresponsible ideas. And to do so, they could act very irresponsibly.

"One of those cars parked along the dock is certainly theirs. Once we know which one, we can do things to it," Charles said.

"What do you propose?" Louise was almost coquettish, holding her face in her hands and tilting her head as she asked this question. Charles denied himself the pleasure of making a joke. He must be tired, Louise thought, realizing that Charles almost never passed up the opportunity to make a play on words or a pun.

"Well, I dunno," he said. "There are the tires, like the President said." They both smiled at the President of the United States suggesting a prank that teenage hooligans might indulge in. "And the gas tank. If it isn't locked, we can mess with the gasoline. If done right, we can damage the engine. And the distributor can usually be altered a little. I'll read up on that before we try anything."

Louise leaned forward. "How about communications?" she said. "We can probably mess with their mail. How do they get mail here? They must have a box at the Post Office," she said answering her own question.

"They certainly have cell phones. How could they coordinate their attack without cell phones?"

Louise nodded enthusiastically. "I'll see if I can find the frequency. Then I'll have to run a decryption algorithm. After that, we can listen in on their conversations. That'll make everything simpler. I might even be able to program the satellite in some way."

"Speaking of listening in," Charles broke in enthusiastically, "we need to get a listening device inside the woonboot. I can place it where they sit when they discuss operations. Their planning will be done there, and we'd miss it if all we heard was their cell phone conversations."

"Can you get in?" Louise wanted to know.

"I can get into the woonboot easily as long as we know no one'll be there for a while." Charles felt confident about his housebreaking skills. "I was thinking too about their food supply, and maybe water. We can probably give them all diarrhea at some point. Or get them all high."

"This is going to be fun," Louise concluded.

"We need to tap into their cell phones first. And get the bug inside."

"I'll get right on the cell phones," Louise added.

They bundled themselves up in their winter gear and left the restaurant feeling that they had had some good ideas, just needing development. The first stage of any operation was exciting; it was the creative part. The train took them quickly to the Central Station, and they walked to their hotel. In the streets around the Central Station, they saw long-haired young people, street musicians, drunks, and other refugees from recent chemical indiscretions. There were also tourists, some of whom were getting caught up in the seamy side of this large, cosmopolitan metropolis. Occasionally there were office workers, policemen, and others who had legitimate business in this area, but they were in the minority.

When they got back to their hotel room, it was still early, but they were tired and eager to sleep, and they fell into the bed. Even so, after lying there for a while, they found that they weren't sleepy after all. One of the difficult things about jet lag was that when you felt tired and wanted to rest, it was often hard to do. Resigning themselves to not sleeping for a while, they put on the TV, where some winter cultural event, a kind of contest, was being broadcast. Louise could tell by the announcer's voice that it was all for laughs, but she couldn't quite figure out what it was that was supposed to be so funny. Charles spoke Dutch fluently and understood what they were doing, but he found it difficult to explain to Louise what the Dutch sense of humor was like. He could explain it, but he couldn't make it funny for her. He gave up trying, and they watched with less and less interest until they felt tired again. This time they fell asleep.

Chapter 3
The Adjustments

Having forgotten to eat dinner the night before, Charles and Louise were hungry for breakfast, and the little pastries at the café weren't enough. Jet lag had attacked their appetites as well as their sleeping habits. They'd sinned against time and were being punished.

In the hotel dining room, an elaborate breakfast was laid out with something for every nationality -- bacon and eggs or pancakes for the Americans, with maple syrup, but not, they noted, the 100% pure variety they liked. The European guests could choose from a variety of cold cuts, cheeses, and small rolls or slices of bread. Above all, the glorious smell of fresh Dutch coffee, strong and black. Charles ate an American breakfast followed by a European one between gulps of hot coffee. Louise was not far behind. More than satisfied, they rode the elevator back to the room, belching discreetly.

Wearing winter coats against the cold they walked to the train station without studying the map. The train was full of sleepy people on the way to work, some trying to get a little more sleep before the day began, their heads nodding as the train rumbled along. Charles and Louise, however, were wide awake. It was three in the afternoon in the States.

The name of the next station was displayed on a digital readout at both ends of the car—a helpful convenience. Even the uninitiated passengers knew where to get off before the train pulled in. This system improved the efficiency of the trains; it wasn't just for the convenience of travelers.

"Why," Charles said, "can't subways in New York City or DC install a system like that?"

"Money, of course," Louise answered in a voice that showed she was interested in keeping Charles company but not much in the digital display.

"Of course," Charles answered. "And in a semi-socialist country like the Netherlands, there's much more to spend on services for the public. Someday Americans are going to appreciate these services and demand them even though it might mean paying a tiny bit more in taxes or train fare."

Louise looked at him. Charles got on these little crusades now and then. Usually they didn't last too long, and they were harmless, she thought. He was, in fact, at this moment calculating the cost per rider of such a system, based on his assumptions of ridership and the supposed cost of the device, neither of which he actually knew, as they exited the train and started to walk toward the woonboot. He didn't really want to know the answer; he was just amused by the process of mental calculation.

"Less than a third of a cent," he said suddenly as they were walking along the quay.

Louise's brow wrinkled momentarily. She'd been thinking about the woonboot. Realizing that Charles had been quiet for some time, she pressed her mind's reverse button until she got back to the last thing he'd said, which was about the cost of that digital display in the train. The wrinkles disappeared.

"Well, that's not enough to worry about, is it?" she said.

"Certainly isn't," Charles said with a note of finality, tinged with self-satisfaction.

They went back to the same little café across the street from the woonboot. The lights were on inside the café, welcoming the predawn traveler. The balding host with the red face welcomed them and took their order for coffee. He recognized them now and greeted them in English, but after a few exchanges in which Charles continued to speak Dutch he responded in kind.

"Where did you learn to speak Dutch so well?" he asked Charles.

Charles had a few stock answers to this question, which he encountered in many different languages in many different countries. Usually, he said that he'd majored in the language in college, but that didn't work for Dutch.

"I lived here a few years ago, doing research," he answered.

The owner nodded as if he understood.

Louise had brought her laptop and began massaging the keyboard as soon as they sat down. Then she put on a pair of earphones and was effectively isolated from her surroundings. The restaurant owner gave her a puzzled look when he came back with two cups of coffee, but Louise took no notice of it, and Charles was intent on the coffee, which at that moment he desperately needed. Louise began to hear conversations in Arabic. She handed the earphones to Charles, to test the information against what they knew about the cell.

"Is this them, do you think?" she asked.

Charles listened carefully. He could hear both sides of the conversation, and after a second to adjust to the new language, he was sure that it was their target group. It would take a little more work, particularly breaking in and planting a listening device, but eventually they'd be able to hear everything in the woonboot, both on and off the cell phones.

Still too full from breakfast to eat anything, they finished their coffee and went outside. As they walked up and down the quay. Charles took note of where the people on the street put their garbage. He identified the can that the terrorists used and after checking to make sure no one was looking, he lifted the lid and peered inside. Just from smelling, he could tell a lot, and later, under cover of darkness he would do a much more thorough examination of what the terrorists threw away. Household trash always provided valuable information as any identity thief knew, but Charles was also figuring out ways to interfere with the woonboot occupants' lives based on the garbage they discarded every day.

Chapter 4
The Men

During the next week they returned to the coffee house several times, to listen in on cell phone conversations and to get their first looks at the men in the woonboot. But after a week of this public spying, the brief commute was too much, and they moved out of their hotel into an apartment on the second floor over the same coffee house. The owner felt somewhat honored to have the two American "journalists" as his tenants in the spare upstairs room.

From the apartment, they could see the woonboot across the street and much of the rest of the dockside area. They settled in, setting up the computer on a little table and erecting a tripod in the window from which Louise could take pictures through her telephoto lens of any activities outside the woonboot. But in fact, during the cold winter days, the men were almost always inside. She did get a very close shot of the face of each one of them as they left the woonboot, which she transmitted to Washington to confirm their identifications.

Over the next several weeks, they listened to the cell phone conversations, accumulating information about the six men and their daily life in Amsterdam. Charles understood Arabic very well and could speak it without an accent, although his vocabulary was not as large as he could wish. He spent a lot of time listening to their cell phone conversations as the terrorists went about their business in the city, traveling to and from the university and shopping. He heard nothing about bombs.

The six men worshipped at a local mosque on Friday nights. On weekends, they shopped at a supermarket a few miles away, driving their little car. From the refuse Charles examined each night in the garbage pail, he could tell that they ate a wide variety, and a large amount, of food. Well, there were six of them and they were young. All of them could drive and they shared the duty of food shopping by taking turns. They went often to the movies. There was one other important form of entertainment that they indulged in. From the conversations they overheard, Charles and Louise discovered that the Saudis, but not the other terrorists, regularly visited Amsterdam's famous red light district. The American terrorist found this distasteful—he had the zealous purity of a convert—and the Kuwaiti pretended to have a girlfriend he visited, but in fact he used these times to contact his American counterpart in the CIA. Later, Charles and Louise discovered more about their Saturday night escapades.

Louise spent a couple of days hacking into their bank accounts. The first thing she discovered was where their money came from. Each month, they received a generous transfer from a bank in Saudi Arabia, and Louise had the number of the account and the name of the bank. She immediately transmitted the information to Henderson who replied that he already knew about it. He reminded them that their job was not to try to shut down the cell but simply to harass the terrorists and make life difficult for them. Perhaps they could make it hard for the guys in the cell to get their money out of the bank, embarrass them, or interfere with their credit rating, ideas that they began to consider immediately.

She also found in their local bank records a complete list of all their bills—phone bills, credit cards, rent, and several single purchases. In Holland, there is no system of checking accounts. Instead, bills are paid directly by the bank, as instructed by the account holder, and a record sent to him. A person making a purchase can also direct the merchant to extract the money directly from their account. The bank records told them a great deal about the movements and daily life of the six men.

Louise's next breakthrough was to tap their cell phone communications more completely. She first listened to their conversations from close to their woonboot, using a device she carried with her that searched for active radio signals. Once she had the signal, she could determine the system they were using, and once into the system she could determine their actual numbers. Then, by communicating directly with the satellite from her own computer, she could reprogram their accounts so that whenever they made a call, or whenever a call was made to one of them, the call would also ring Charles' phone and at the same time stream the signal to her computer to keep a record. They could hear and record everything the six men said on their cell phones.

Food and water, housing, transportation, money and communication were the main areas of vulnerability, but Charles also wondered if he might mess a little with some of their most deeply held beliefs. It might make some of their other tricks more disconcerting.

Four of the six men were, according to Henderson, using their real names, something other terrorists had also done. The three brothers—Akhmed, Muhammad, and Osama—shared the surname al-Ryadi, a name that Charles and Louise had encountered before in their adventures in Kazakhstan. They wondered if there was a connection. Perhaps these young men were relatives of the man in Kazakhstan who had funded suicide bombings until their work resulted in his arrest. The cousin's name was Ibrahim, also al-Ryadi. The Kuwaiti gave his name as Talgat al-Iraqi. Calling himself "al-Iraqi" had probably helped in convincing the brothers and the cousin of his authenticity. It was, of course, not his real name. And the American, whose real name was Arthur Penderley, called himself Anwar al-Jihadi, the Warrior, also to establish his authenticity as a terrorist.

As Charles and Louise listened in on their conversations, a pattern to their lives began to emerge. All the men had student visas, and according to the Dutch law they were required them to attend a university in the Netherlands, which they all did. They were enrolled and they each faithfully attended classes at the Vrije Universiteit Amsterdam. In addition, they were obligated to study both Dutch and English and to reach a certain level of proficiency in Dutch by a certain date or lose their visas. But this requirement was not a problem. The standards of proficiency were low, they were all young and quick to learn languages, and they were all exposed to both Dutch and English often, Dutch because that was what people here spoke, and English because most Dutch people knew the language and were quick to use it if they suspected someone of being foreign, which happened frequently to the five dark-skinned, black-haired Arabic men. The same thing, however, happened to the American, who with brown hair, blue eyes, and fair skin, did not look Arabic, but did speak Dutch with an American accent, which the Dutch knew well, and to which they responded in English.

Chapter 5
The Voice

The local people were friendly and accommodating to the six men. The Dutch are typically open and forthright, but beyond this they were strongly opposed to American interference in the Middle East and as a result they were particularly friendly to Arabs. Had they known, however, that these six men were now prepared to attack the World Court in The Hague, which the Dutch were very proud to have housed in their country, their friendliness would have disappeared like water through an open sluice.

On Saturday, the six terrorists relaxed, separating into groups. The three brothers were always together, sometimes including the cousin. The Kuwaiti mole tried to spend time with the Saudis, but he could tell that they often didn't want his company, so he held back, not wanting to push his luck. As a result, he was often in the company of the American, which he saw as an opportunity to monitor the more radical views the American held.

On Saturdays, the Saudis typically went to a bar and drank for a few hours, after which they went to the red light district and engaged prostitutes. Charles and Louise had been exposed to various types of Muslims in their work, but had found very few who honored the prohibitions against alcohol and fornication, although most of the Muslims they had known, even those with only loosely held beliefs, were appalled or sickened at the thought of eating pork. The Saturday night drinking and whoring provided a relatively long period of time when the woonboot was empty, and Charles and Louise decided to exploit the opportunity.

One Saturday night, when the men were partying in the central part of Amsterdam, Charles walked over to the woonboot. Outside on the quay, he found a piling on which he planted a transponder inconspicuously next to a cleat. This transponder was larger than the one he would plant inside the woonboot and would boost the signal and transmit it for several hundred meters, enabling Louise to pick it up with clarity on her computer in the apartment over the coffeehouse. Then he crossed over the quayside woonboot and stepped onto the terrorists' deck. He found his way through the lock without difficulty, opened the hatch door, and eased himself down the stairs.

He found himself in a common room furnished with second-hand chairs and a sofa, gathered around a television set. He could imagine them holding a meeting there if they needed to discuss something or come to a common agreement. He placed a small transponder under the sofa on the inside surface high up on one of the legs. It was the most central location he could find where discovery was unlikely. He considered planting a second device, just for backup, but realized that if one of the devices were discovered it would surely prompt a complete search of the whole place, which would uncover the second device anyway.

Next, he looked over the rest of the woonboot to get a sense of what it was like, and he carefully smelled each bed to get the personal scent of each terrorist. He had a method of cataloguing scents mentally, which he now used, carefully establishing a category for the beds. He knew then that he could recognize any of the terrorists in the dark, or if he was blindfolded. Then, he checked to make sure that the listening device was working by calling on his cell phone the number that connected him to Louise's computer and making a few noises himself. When he heard the sounds that he generated inside the woonboot being recorded on Louise's system, he knew everything was ready, and he let himself out the way he'd come in and locked the hatch behind him. Outside, he crossed quietly back over the inner woonboot and then walked nonchalantly back to their apartment. It was a relief to get out of "enemy territory" without being discovered, and he felt that they would get all the information they needed between the cell phone conversations and those that took place inside the woonboot.

He reported his findings to Louise.

"There's a main room where they watch television, and where they can all sit. It's where they will meet to discuss anything of importance. I put the bug under the sofa, on one of the legs, so you might hear some sounds like feet kicking the sofa leg, or pants cuffs rubbing against the sofa leg, maybe even footsteps. I don't think these noises will interfere with speech."

"OK. Is there any danger of them kicking the device off?" she asked.

"I don't think so. It's on the back side of the sofa leg. To kick it off, they'd have to wrap a toe around the sofa leg. And it is up high against the underside of the sofa, so it's unlikely that they'll see it while cleaning."

"They probably won't clean very thoroughly," Louise commented, "and maybe not at all. They certainly won't hire someone to come in and clean."

Charles went on. "There are two sleeping rooms toward the front of the woonboot, one on either side of the central walkway, and in the very front is the bathroom. Toward the back, are two other sleeping rooms, again one on either side of the central walkway. Then there is another room farther back. It looks as though it was originally a place where someone might work on engine repair or other repair work. It smelled of lubricating oil. But there is a bed in it now. Judging by the smell, it's the American who sleeps there."

"How can you tell that?" Louise asked incredulously.

"I can't really. It is just a hunch. Maybe it's the soap he uses or some difference in his diet. But the bed in that room smelled to me more like an American had been sleeping in it."

"OK. It probably won't make any difference who is in which bed anyway."

"Probably not."

"As I think about it, that bed and one of the other ones toward the rear lacked the smell of women's perfume, which I could detect faintly in all the other beds. It probably comes from the prostitutes."

"Well, they don't have any maiden aunties living in Amsterdam," she said.

"I have a technical question," Charles asked Louise with a gleam in his eye, "the way the cell phone tap is arranged, can we talk to them, or can we only listen?"

"I have it set up so that we can only listen. It makes it safer for us; a sneeze or cough or hiccup could tip them off that they're being listened to," she answered.

"Yes, of course. That makes sense. Can you change it on one phone, just temporarily, so that we can talk to them without calling them?" He was smiling, and she knew that he had something particularly mischievous in mind, but she didn't ask him about it. Louise liked being toyed with.

"Why don't you just call them? We know their numbers."

"Later on, I'll do that. But I want the first contact to come out of nowhere. It'll be more mysterious that way."

"Sure, I can do that. I just have to send some code to the satellite. I'll set it up so that you enter a code before you place the call, and it will automatically revert to one-way when you hang up." She looked at him in a way that was a little flirtatious, wondering what he was thinking of doing.

"I love it when you talk techy like that," he said, responding to her flirtatiousness.

Louise smiled. Usually, she appreciated Charles' sense of humor.

"Which phone do you want to speak on?" she asked.

"Ibrahim's." Charles had already decided to try something a little different.

"Give me a little time."

She went to work and in a few minutes, had reprogrammed the cousin's phone tap so that Charles could call him. Charles waited at the window of their apartment, watching the woonboot, until the cousin and the three brothers were just entering. Then he called the cousin.

"With Ibrahim," said the Saudi, answering in Dutch, and in the Dutch manner, with a short version of "You are speaking with Ibrahim."

Charles adopted a sepulchral tone and said in a flowery Arabic that had the flavor of holy writ, "Thou disappointest me, Ibrahim." He used the familiar pronoun—the equivalent of "thou"—to make himself sound paternal and authoritarian. He hung up before Ibrahim had a chance even to ask who it was.

Later in the evening, the four men left the woonboot, and Charles figured that, because it was Saturday, they were on their way to the red light district. He didn't follow them, but he made sure that he was on the same train, in another car. At the stop for the red light district, Charles got off and was pleased to see that the Saudis also got off the train and were headed with lustful determination toward the exit. Charles followed them onto the street where he stopped from time to time to look at various women. Some of them smiled at him and beckoned for him to come inside, but he just shook his head and moved on to another window, watching the Saudis at the other end of the street. They walked up and down the street looking at the women displayed in the windows like the goods they were. Two of the brothers made their decision and entered a door. The cousin was next. When he rang the doorbell of one of the prostitutes, Charles called again. He was startled but he answered the phone.

"Again thou disappointest me Ibrahim."

Then he hung up. He waited for a half hour until the cousin emerged, looking furtively up and down the street. Charles, however, moved around a corner out of sight as soon as he saw the man step outside. Then he called again.

"Ibrahim, Ibrahim. How can you hurt me so?" This time he stayed on the line.

"Who is this?" The Saudi tried to sound indignant, but his voice was shaking.

"Thou knowest. And thou knowest thy behavior is wrong. I am afraid there must be consequences."

"Who is this? Who is calling?" But there was no answer. Charles had hung up and was hurrying to catch a train.

Ibrahim al-Ryadi went home unusually silent that night. He said nothing to his cousin, or anyone, about what he'd heard. He was disturbed and upset. He wondered first if perhaps he had imagined the calls. He was aware of feeling guilty about visiting the prostitutes and wondered if guilt could produce hallucinations. He thought too of talking to the Imam at the mosque. There he could have described his feelings of guilt and his worries about the calls, but to do so would have meant confessing his behavior, which he was afraid to do. He knew that a confession would result in a very scathing rebuke, a tongue-lashing in fact. Maybe he deserved such a rebuke; he thought that at least he would stop feeling guilty, but the fact of the matter was that he didn't want to stop going to the prostitutes, and he knew that if he talked to the Imam he'd have to make a promise to give up his Saturday night excursions.

What he really wanted to discuss with the Imam was the possibility that he was being called by a higher power. Could it be? Who would believe him if he said he was talking to the Prophet, or maybe even Allah himself—he shuddered at the thought—on a cell phone? He did not believe it himself, he argued mentally. On the other hand, who knew how these cell phones worked? There was he knew, a satellite high in the heavens, beyond his sight... he shuddered again. Anything was possible with Allah.

Chapter 6
The Sickness

Charles then set about creating a small set of plagues for the six men. Where possible, he focused on the cousin. He asked Louise to fiddle with the cousin's bank account so that the latest transfer did not appear. Their bills were paid, but soon there appeared to be, from the bank's point of view, no money in the account, and the bank called the cousin and asked him to drop by for a visit, which he did. He was embarrassed to be told that he would have to make a deposit before they could finish paying his bills. He argued that transfers had been made, enough to cover all of their expenses, but he had no confirming evidence because the transfers had all been electronic. Meanwhile, he called "Uncle" (the only name they knew him by) who was his contact in Saudi Arabia, and "Uncle" assured him that a transfer had been made.

"Please check with your bank, Uncle, because they say here that no money has been received."

"I will do so," came the cryptic reply, followed by the decisive click that terminated the connection.

But of course, when he checked with his bank, "Uncle" found that according to his records the money had been sent. He called Ibrahim and told him as much. Charles had already asked Louise to reinstate the money. They didn't want the banks to begin an investigation. So, when Ibrahim, filled with righteous anger, went to the bank to complain, he found them apologetic and confused. The money was there where it was supposed to be. As he came out of the bank, Charles again called him on the phone, and again used his deepest voice.

"I said there would be consequences. That was only the first. It will not be the least." Then he hung up.

Charles and Louise had been watching them carefully for some time and had noticed a lapse in their movements that could be exploited. The six men took turns shopping for food, and when they brought the food home in their small car, they left the car unlocked for the few minutes it took them to carry the first armloads of shopping bags across the first woonboot and into theirs. There was then, perhaps a minute or less, when the part of their food supply that was in the second load was vulnerable. Having discovered this, Charles and Louise prepared themselves and waited patiently in the café for the car to arrive from the shopping trip, which took place always on Monday afternoon. It was this time the American, and he followed the usual pattern. As soon as he'd disappeared inside the woonboot, Charles and Louise came out into the street. Louise carried a hypodermic needle filled with water in which they had carefully cultured bacteria taken from the toilet in their own apartment. Charles popped open the trunk, and Louise looked inside. She spread the tops of each bag, found a melon in one, and injected it. Then the meat. Charles closed the trunk and they walked away, back to their apartment, listening behind them as the American reappeared for the second load. It had not taken more than three minutes for them to create considerable chaos during the next few days.

They must have eaten one of contaminated products that night, for there were no phone calls at all the following day, and on the direct speaker hooked up to the listening device Charles had planted they heard only groans and frequent flushing. On Wednesday, a call came in for one of them. It was a Jordanian girl who had befriended one of the Saudis after a shared class, enquiring if they were OK, since none of them had been seen for a couple of days at the university. The weak voice in response said they were all very sick, although there was some improvement. They might return to classes on Friday. Later that day, their Dutch language tutor called, and there was a similar conversation.

On Thursday morning, Charles called Ibrahim.

"Thou seest, Ibrahim, that I control thy bowels and all parts of thee. There will be one more consequence."

"No, no, please. We will not go to the bar or to the prostitutes."

"Good. I am pleased. But still, there will be one more."

"Oh God," moaned Ibrahim.

"Exactly," said Charles and hung up.

The next night, when they were all sleeping, finally, after gaining ground on their intestinal infections, Charles and Louise poured two liters of water into their gas tank.

***

On Friday, all six of them got up slowly, feeling within themselves for signs of the sickness. Cautiously, they got ready to go back to school, dressing slowly, checking the color of their faces in the mirror and wondering if they should try to eat anything. None of them had any appetite, but they also knew that their feeling of weakness was partly caused by their lack of nutrition. But the thought of food was repulsive. The diarrhea had stopped, but their stomachs were still sore.

Ibrahim said nothing to them about the mysterious calls he'd received. He was still not sure what to make of them. He didn't think they were a trick. He thought perhaps there was a malfunction in the phone, but that seemed very unlikely. As much as he turned it around in his mind, the most likely explanation was that he'd incurred the wrath of God. The voice that he heard sounded authentic, even down to the Koranic style of Arabic. How else could one explain it? It made him very nervous too—he did feel guilty for his behavior—and no matter how much he thought about it, the best explanation was that he had offended Allah. If that were true, he knew what to do. He must pray and he must stop drinking and whoring.

They all got in the car and drove to school without difficulty. Osama drove because he felt strongest. He had no way of knowing that the gasoline was floating on top of two liters of water. The gas gauge, floating high, said that the tank was full. They parked the car with difficulty; parking spaces in Amsterdam were very scarce, and they had to drive around for nearly a half hour before they came upon someone just leaving one. It was small and they had to try several times before they managed to squeeze the car into the space.

They were already a few minutes late for class, but they couldn't hurry. The weakness they felt made them all walk slowly and carefully. They arrived at the lecture hall quite late and entered as quietly as they could, but they were a large group, and many of the students, already bored with the lecture, turned to see what the disturbance was. The Arabs separated quickly and found seats far apart from each other, embarrassed by the disturbance.

They found it hard to concentrate. They kept checking inwardly to assess the state of their bowels. Listening to a lecture in Dutch, which none of them yet spoke with fluency, was difficult under the best of circumstances, and now, with this added distraction, it was impossible. They took notes, but missed large sections of material, and knew they'd have to spend extra time, back in the woonboot, comparing their notes to make sure all the information was written down. By the end of the class, they were desperate to go to the bathroom. They didn't really have diarrhea any more, but they needed to make sure. Afterwards they rallied outside the men's room, looked at each other with pain and fatigue and walked slowly to their car.

They drove home without difficulty. There was still enough gasoline floating on top of the water for the engine to use, and the valve where the gasoline entered the fuel line leading to the engine was a little more than halfway up the tank. Once, the engine sputtered slightly. They had gone around a left-hand turn, which lowered the level of gas in the tank on the left side, where the valve was, but as soon as they were around the corner, gasoline began to flow to the engine again, and the car ran well. They had no trouble parking in their residential neighborhood, and they walked to the woonboot. Inside, they all fell into their beds, craving rest. It was Friday night and they hoped they would feel rested enough to go to the mosque for prayers. They all felt the need for more strength.

They got up after an hour or so of rest, fed themselves cautiously, and made sure their appearance would not be an affront to the Prophet. Once again, they walked slowly to the car. They were getting stronger, but recovery was slow.

The car started and they pulled out into the street, but after they'd driven a few blocks, it died quickly. The frustration they felt, on top of their fatigue and weakness, made it hard to deal with the situation. Ibrahim was more than frustrated; he was nervous. He needed to go to the mosque—a new feeling for him. Usually, Friday night prayers were a kind of ritual. They looked forward to them because their religious heritage made them feel like a part of a larger enterprise; it gave them perspective. It also helped them feel justified in their mission. On this night they would have gained a sense of strength. They would have come away feeling a little healthier, a little more supported in their endeavors. But it wasn't going to happen.

The car would not restart, and after many attempts, and hearing the starter motor getting weaker, they knew that the battery was dying, and they called for a tow truck.

Then there was a long wait. They all sat limply in the car while they waited. When the truck came, they had the usual difficulty communicating with the driver as they struggled with the Dutch language. Eventually they explained what had happened and the car was towed to a service station. Then, again, they had the problem with the language, but after looking up some words in the Dutch/Arabic dictionaries that they all carried, they succeeded in explaining the problem to the attendant, who told them that they'd have to leave the car there. They walked weakly to the nearest train station, following the attendant's directions.

It was getting late by this time, and the trains were not running as frequently, so they had to wait for a while on the platform. When the train came, they all slumped onto the seats, closing their eyes in fatigue, but they didn't sleep. They had to change trains once, and go through another wait on another platform before finally boarding the train that would take them to their last stop. It was after 10 when they finally got back and fell into bed.

They slept late the next morning. It was Saturday and they had no classes. The phone rang in midmorning, waking them all. Ibrahim was closest to the phone, but he didn't want to answer it, and he gestured to Akhmed to take the call. Akhmed gave him a puzzled look but took the call. It was the service station, and Akhmed listened carefully to the Dutch, stopping occasionally to ask one of his cohorts for the meaning of a word. In time, it became clear to them that the mechanics at the service station had drained the gas tank and found a large quantity of water in the tank. They had examined the tank carefully and could find no way for water to get into it, even in small quantities, except through the filling port, which meant that someone had put the water in.

They were baffled at first, then angry. The service people said that someone had to have put it there.

"Who would do this?" asked Akhmed.

"There are many hooligans in this country," said Osama.

"It's the neighborhood boys. They do not like Arabs," offered Talgat.

"Perhaps we could keep watch," suggested Muhammad.

Ibrahim was quiet, as was Anwar. Ibrahim knew what the problem was. God didn't like their behavior. They weren't following the laws of the Prophet, and they would be punished for it. He knew that much. What he didn't know was when it would stop. He hoped it would be soon, but he was afraid that his cousins wouldn't stop their sinful behavior, and the plagues would continue. Anwar, cynical and wise in the ways of the world, wasn't sure, but he wondered if they were being sabotaged by agents from the US or the Dutch government.

Chapter 7
The Phones

None of them wanted to go out the following night. Too weak from the illness to enjoy fleshly pursuits, and repulsed at the thought of alcohol or anything strongly flavored getting into their sore and sensitive intestines, they wanted to sit quietly in their woonboot and watch TV. Talgat wondered when he would get a chance to call his counterpart at the CIA. It would have to wait.

Ibrahim, however, decided to reform. He made a vow—to himself and also to his Cell Phone Caller—that he would never again drink or visit prostitutes. He began to think about his cousins too. He wouldn't try to convince them, at least not directly, which might reveal his motives, but he decided that the next time a trip to the bar or the red light district was suggested, he would be less enthusiastic, even beg off, using an excuse. Eventually, he thought, he could say that these pleasures no longer appealed to him. And then, a little later, he could remind them of the prohibitions in holy scripture. It was a kind of plan, and he was glad of it. He felt the zeal of the reformer—that he was doing God's work. With such thoughts kept to himself, or at least between himself and God, he could go to the mosque and pray with a free spirit. And he hoped, he fervently hoped, that there would be no more afflictions.

"I'm pleased," Charles said as they cradled their after-breakfast coffee cups. "There was a tremor in Ibrahim's voice on the phone. And did you see his furtive glances in the red light district?"

Louise nodded. "It's promising," she said. "Do you want to try the same thing with one of the others?"

"Not now," Charles said. "We have to be careful. If they begin to compare notes, we might be discovered."

"Of course," Louise chimed in. "They'll see that someone's messing with them, and then they'll be suspicious of everything else we might do."

"OK then. No more calls from God," Charles concluded.

"I'm more interested in slowing them down, making it hard for them to move around, do business, communicate," Louise said, trying to come up with additional ideas.

"Communication," Charles said decisively. "That's already a source of frustration with them. What do you have in mind?"

"I hear a note of fiendish glee in your voice," Louise said, tilting her head coquettishly.

"I know your technical skill," he answered. "I'm sure you'll come up with something appropriately diabolical."

"I can program the satellite in various ways, just to slow them down, frustrate their purposes," Louise offered.

"I haven't thought out the details yet," she went on, "but I can monkey with the way their cell phones work."

"That's what we're here for," Charles agreed.

Louise sat down at the computer and accessed the satellite. She then sent code to the satellite so that on every 2nd, 3rd or 4th call each of them made—she told the satellite to vary the interval—their phone would hang up after ten seconds. A few calls would go through, but many would be lost. They used the cell phones often, calling each other whenever they were separated to coordinate their travel and meeting. The hang-ups would slow them down.

The next day, Muhammad was leaving a class in Dutch history and called Ibrahim, who had driven that morning, to arrange for a ride home. It would save him from a walk to the Central Station in the city and a shorter walk to the woonboot. He first called Talgat, who was in another class and told him what he was doing, then he called Ibrahim.

The phone rang and rang. Muhammad had already noticed that Ibrahim did not like to answer the phone. He had seen him shy away from answering the landline in the woonboot and now he could tell that Ibrahim's cell phone was ringing but was not being picked up. After eight rings—Muhammad counted them—Ibrahim answered in a hesitant and somewhat quavering voice.

"With Ibrahim." They tried to speak Dutch whenever they might be talking to a Dutch person.

"Are you all right?" Muhammad asked in Arabic, a little impatiently.

"Yes, yes, I am fine."

"Then why do you wait so long..." He heard the suddenly profound silence that meant that the connection had been broken.

"Damn! What is the matter with this phone?" He dialed again, but this time he received a busy signal. He hung up again, and as soon as he had done so, the phone rang. It was Ibrahim.

"What happened?" Ibrahim asked.

"I don't know. The connection suddenly went dead."

"What did you want?" Ibrahim was a little impatient. He wanted to get off the phone as soon as possible.

"I was asking..." Muhammad, frustrated, decided not to ask the question that he had begun to ask Ibrahim. "Never mind. Where are you?"

"I am on the Prinsengracht, heading toward the car."

"Can you wait in the car? I'll be there in a few minutes. The class just got out."

"Sure, I'll wait."

Ibrahim reached the car and got in behind the steering wheel. It would have been useful to call the rest of the group and tell them he was waiting so they could all ride home together, but he didn't. He didn't want to make the phone call.

In a while Osama called Ibrahim, wanting to know where he was, and Ibrahim told him that he was waiting in the car. He suggested that he call Akhmed and find out where he was and if he was free to meet them at the car.

Osama placed the call and heard Akhmed answer, but before he could relay Ibrahim's message to him, the line went suddenly dead. He gave a mild curse—Osama was the most patient of the three brothers and was not easily upset—then called again, connected with Akhmed, and relayed Ibrahim's message.

After that, he gave up. He could have called Anwar and Talgat too, but they would find their way home by train. Anwar was very stoic and Talgat was a Kuwaiti, which meant that there was a little less likelihood of the Saudi brothers including him in their plans. The phone frustration had just brought out the ethnic separation between them.

When they were all back at the woonboot, Muhammad and Osama complained about the difficulties they'd experienced with the phone.

"Maybe there is something wrong with the way it is set up," suggested Anwar, always practical in his American way. "If you take it back to the store where you bought it, they will check it out for you."

The next day they had no classes and went to the electronics store in the Central Station, where they'd bought the phones.

"They suddenly cut off?" the store clerk asked. "That is peculiar. Let me try."

He clicked out the number of a friend, and the call went through without difficulty.

"It seems to be working properly," he said.

"But yesterday it did not," countered Akhmed. "Something was wrong with it."

"I can't find anything wrong with it now. But sometimes the signal from the satellite is broken. It may be from the weather or sunspots or something. Just try the call again."

They retrieved their phones from the store clerk, dissatisfied and a little angry at Anwar for suggesting that they try to get the store to fix the problem. They'd wasted a few hours of the morning when they could have been studying.

The occasional and unpredictable difficulty with the phones continued. They would curse and make the call a second time. It would almost always work on the second try, and sometimes on the first try, so after a while they just came to accept that the phones did not work as well as they should. It became a practice for them to mutter "Insha'a Allah"—if God wills it—before they placed a call. Their phone bill increased, but not by very much, and their "Uncle" in Riyadh was paying the bills anyway, so it didn't matter.

Chapter 8
The Bank

Their car had been repaired, although at considerable expense. The mechanics had drained the entire fuel line, then flushed it out with gasoline plus a cleansing additive. The water had been in the line only for a short while, but there was nonetheless a small effect on the surface of the pistons and cylinders. The car ran, but it didn't run as well as it used to; probably, there was some minor pitting to the cylinders, which reduced compression. When, after a few days, they took it out on the highway, they discovered that it would not go much faster than 40 mph, which was way too slow for driving on the local highways, where the Dutch drivers often went 80 mph, and the German drivers passing through the Netherlands on their way to the beach would often drive at 100 or 120, paying the fines as if they were part of the cost of doing business.

The occupants of the woonboot began to look for another car, and at car dealers on the outskirts of Amsterdam, they quickly found one that suited their purposes. The cost of the car, however, was more than their bank account could manage. They conferred among themselves.

"Why don't we just email "Uncle" and have him send the money?" Osama suggested.

"It is the simplest thing to do," said Akhmed.

"But we are supposed to act like ordinary citizens, not the rich children of oil sheiks," argued Anwar. "We should take out a loan from a bank just as anyone else would do."

"The American is right," said Ibrahim. "We do not want to leave evidence of large sums of money being sent to us from home. It might look suspicious. Besides, Uncle might not be willing."

So Ibrahim and Akhmed together went to a neighborhood bank and applied for a loan.

Louise, however, found it quite easy to modify their credit history to include a number of bad debts and a repossession. The bank turned down their loan application but did not offer any explanation. They went to another bank, and then another one, but were each time refused the loan.

One of the loan officers finally showed them the credit report.

"You can see here, with a repossession and these delinquencies no bank will give you a loan. You will have to find cash to buy your car."

Akhmed exploded "But we have never taken out a loan before! How could we have defaulted?"

The loan officer, somewhat used to people being angry when they could not get money that they needed, simply raised his hands and shook his head slowly.

"I do not know *Meneer*."

"Do you hear me? We could not possibly have such a record! It is a mistake!" His voice became louder and louder. The loan officer surreptitiously pressed a button under his desk, and the bank security guard, who had heard the raised voices even through the closed door, decided that it would be a good idea to call the police. He was not sure that he trusted these Arab types. Ibrahim tried to calm his cousin.

"It is just a mistake. We will take care of it." He was not sure it was a mistake of human origin, but he saw, rightly enough, that he had to calm Akhmed down.

Akhmed continued to protest in a loud voice. The frustrations of the last few days were beginning to take a toll on him, and it was difficult for him to argue a case without losing his temper. Hearing Ibrahim, he tried to calm himself down.

"Look, all I am trying to say is that there must be a mistake in the record!" He began this sentence calmly but by the time he had reached the end of it, his voice was loud again.

"I am going to have to ask you to leave the bank," said the loan officer who felt that it was important to get them out of the building. There were other customers to think of. He got up and went to the door, opened it, and gestured for the security guard to come in. Akhmed did not want at all to have an altercation, particularly one with an armed guard, so he gently put his hand on the loan officer's arm. This was a mistake. The loan officer, already frightened a little by the shouting, which this excitable man did not seem to be able to control, jerked away in a small panic. Akhmed immediately tried to apologize, but his Dutch was not good, and he became frustrated at his inability to communicate.

The police came into the bank, guns drawn and serious. A disturbance in a bank could mean many things. There had been a number of hostage situations that had occurred in banks and there was always the possibility of robbery. The security guard directed them to the office. The door was open and a middle-eastern looking man was trying to explain something to the bank officer. His voice was low, but it was easy for the police officers to hear the tension in it. They interrupted him and asked him to explain himself. He had to start all over, and it was impossible for him to keep completely calm. The officers asked him to step back, farther away from the bank officer. They were worried that a hostage situation could develop under their noses. Then they asked the bank officer to tell his side of the story.

"I was asking these men to leave, because they were yelling and disturbing the customers, when this one"—he pointed to Akhmed—"grabbed me."

The policeman looked at Akhmed. "Did you grab him?"

"I only touched his arm. I was trying to..."

"OK, I am going to have to remove you from the scene. Please turn around."

"But it is…"

"Just turn around, please."

Akhmed did as he was told, and the policeman placed handcuffs on him and searched him thoroughly, which Akhmed found extremely insulting. His mood became surly, and when the policeman took him by the arm to lead him out of the bank, he jerked his arm away. The policeman stopped and faced him.

"You will do as I say or I will have you charged with resisting arrest."

"Please do as he says," said Ibrahim.

At that Akhmed meekly acquiesced and allowed himself to be led from the bank and placed in a squad car.

"May I come too?" asked Ibrahim.

"Who are you?"

"I am this man's cousin," he said, not sure if it was enough but not wanting to say any more than necessary. The situation had already gotten out of hand, and Ibrahim knew that he would have to send some kind of report to Uncle.

The policeman agreed, and Ibrahim got in the police car, in the back seat, next to Akhmed. They were driven quickly to a nearby police station, where they were both interviewed and fingerprinted. Ibrahim began to worry. What if their fingerprints were already on record somewhere? Indeed, their identities were checked by computer as a matter of routine even while they were being interviewed, and the police soon knew that they had arrested two members of a known terrorist cell. A quick phone call was made to a Dutch security agent, who made another phone call to the American embassy. The Americans suggested that the men be let go. They had not done anything serious. They were already under very close surveillance. There was no point in inflaming this incident. The message was relayed, and in less than half an hour the policemen knew what they must do.

Ibrahim, Akhmed, and the interviewing police detective were sitting in a room reserved for interrogation when the door opened and another policeman, dressed in plain clothes, walked in.

OK, *heren*, you are free to go," he said. "But in the future you will need to control your tempers. Here in Holland, we do not yell at the people we are asking to borrow money from." He smiled knowingly as he said this, and it served, quite contrary to his purpose, to infuriate the Arabs even more. They were being lectured to like children when in fact the problem had begun because of an error the bank had made.

This event troubled them. The last thing they wanted was to become known to law enforcement, and it had happened. They had been arrested, fingerprinted, and interrogated. Of course, they had said that they were students seeking asylum and education. But as they left the police station, aware that they had broken a major rule taught to them in training, they were beginning to doubt their ability to be jihadis.

Chapter 9
The Poison Pen

Louise was pleased. Charles heard over the bug line the two terrorists describing what had happened to them, and he could tell that their confidence had fallen. After he translated the whole conversation to Louise, she agreed.

She then put their next operation into effect. She wrote an anonymous letter to the instructor of a course that Akhmed, Osama, and the American were taking on the history of the Netherlands. Pretending to be another student in the class, she told the instructor that she had become friends with them and discovered that they were cheating on the weekly quizzes the instructor gave. She made it clear that she did not appreciate being shown up as a result of cheating by others. She wrote that the three had developed a system of signals they used to send each other the correct answers to the multiple choice questions, and she described some of the signals, using gestures and mannerisms that were common among the three men. Akhmed, for example, often ran his hand through his short-cropped hair, particularly when he was thinking or trying to remember something, and she informed the instructor that this meant the third choice. Scratching the nose meant the first, and there were several others that she described, but she didn't know all of the signals, she wrote. Before signing off, she added that she hoped the instructor would take some action to stop the cheating that was having a personal effect on her own grades.

During the next quiz, the instructor watched the men carefully and saw them "signaling" to each other.

"Meneer Al-Ryadi, and…" She consulted her attendance sheet, "ah, I see Akhmed al-Ryadi and Osama al-Ryadi, and, and, Meneer Al-Jihadi, please see me after class."

They looked at each other and shrugged quizzically, but got up and went down to her lectern.

"Gentlemen, I realize that you are not accustomed to our Dutch ways, so I will forgive your indiscretions this time."

"Excuse me?" Anwar, the American, did not find it difficult to confront a professor. "What indiscretions?

"I have seen you signaling to each other," she said.

"We are not signaling to each other!" Anwar said, changing to English and raising his voice.

Osama put his hand on Anwar's shoulder. "Brother, please…"

"No! We were not signaling anything."

"I am sorry, but it was quite evident to me, and…" She hesitated. "Other students have noticed too."

"What? That is not possible," said Anwar, again in English. "Who are these students? They are trying to gain an advantage!"

"I don't think so," said the professor after a pause, but her confidence somewhat shaken as she realized the possibility, which had not occurred to her before.

"Brother, please," said Osama. "We should not make this situation worse."

"You must realize that you are no longer in Yemen, where there are apparently different customs."

"You are right about that," said Osama quietly but with an edge in his voice. "But we are not from Yemen, and…"

"Oh, I am sorry to have presumed… many people of your, your…" She searched vainly for a word that would not be insulting. "Many refugees have come from Yemen."

"I see," said Osama, gripping Anwar's arm a little more tightly as he felt his muscles tense. "I believe we will have to file a complaint against you with the Dean's office."

"Yes!" said Anwar, a little too loudly. "And we will need the name of the student who spoke to you."

"I am afraid I do not have that name. The complaint came in an anonymous note. Please, can we not just drop the matter?"

"No!" shouted Anwar.

"Yes!" said Osama turning on Anwar. "We will drop the matter."

"But..."

"Please," said Osama to Anwar. "It is for the best."

Anwar turned without saying anything and walked toward the door.

"Thank you," Osama said politely. "We will not pursue the matter with the Dean's Office, but perhaps, in the future..."

"Yes, of course," said the professor, reaching out to shake his hand.

"I may not touch you," Osama said coldly. Then he nodded at Akhmed, whose face was still bright red, and turned to leave.

Anwar was waiting for them in the doorway, and as they all exited, he said "Bitch!" just loudly enough for the professor to hear. Her face darkened and she bent over her desk to write down their names. "I should report this incident myself," she said quietly.

The following week there was another quiz, and once again the teacher watched the three men carefully and observed them "signaling" again. Again she asked them to stay after class and again she gave them a stern lecture about cheating. Although they were trembling with anger and frustration, they were able to make the teacher consider the possibility that their movements during the quiz were innocent.

The teacher then began to consider the possibility that the letter she had received was a hoax, sent perhaps by a jilted girlfriend. For the first time she took a close look at the students' answers on the quiz and found that they could not have been signaling answers to each other. There was some similarity in the pattern of their answers, but they studied together, as they had explained to her, which explained the similarity, but there were also differences between their answers, enough so that she thought it unlikely that they were cheating. She read and reread the letter, but she could find no clue in it that helped identify the sender. She was also embarrassed that she had not looked more carefully at their quizzes in the first place, so it was easiest not to retract her original comments or apologize for them, but to simply drop the whole matter. She decided not to report the incident.

"I guess we can close the 'poisoned pen' operation," Charles said, as the two agents lingered over their morning coffee.

"Definitely," Louise agreed.

"Was it a success, do you think?" Charles asked.

"I don't think so. We succeeded in embarrassing and frustrating the terrorists, but it didn't slow them down or interfere with their mission, as far as I can tell."

"No, I guess not," Charles agreed. "Before you woke up this morning, I listened to the recordings of their conversations last night in the woonboot." Charles paused, thinking.

"Well?" Louise prompted.

"I'm thinking."

"OK."

"They sounded frustrated and angry, particularly at the bank and the police, but more generally at the Dutch people, and their language, which has not been easy for them to learn."

"Sure," said Louise. "But I'm not sure that is helpful to us. It will increase their motivation to act against the Dutch."

"So, the operation has backfired," Charles concluded.

"Well, I don't know. Maybe not entirely."

"Why not?"

"All the anger and frustration might make them act more rashly, or do something stupid."

"So, maybe Uncle would call them off completely?"

"It's a possibility."

"But remote, I think."

"Probably."

"We won't try anything like that again, I guess."

"No," said Louise thoughtfully. "But maybe we should go in the other direction."

"And that means..." Charles left the sentence hanging.

"Instead of bolstering their hatred, maybe we could, I don't know, help one of them fall in love."

Charles laughed out loud. "Maybe that would work. Love can seriously disrupt a person's life."

"You would know," Louise added sarcastically.

"Right," Charles said, considering his own history of disruptive relationships.

"If we could arrange for a meeting between one of the guys and some lovely young thing, maybe it would make a few sparks fly. Then human nature and youthful hormones could do the rest."

"I like the idea. A Love Campaign. It's worth a try."

They puttered around during the day, checking their instruments and listening to chatter in the woonboot. They did some shopping in the afternoon, and ate in one of Amsterdam's better restaurants. Then went home, still thoughtful, but ready for a good night's sleep.

"Let's get away for a while," Louise suggested the next morning as they sat again in the café for breakfast.

"Any particular reason?" asked Charles.

"Just to get away..." She hesitated. "A new environment will help us reconsider everything. Think in a new way," Louise offered as she crunched a large bite of crispy toast.

"Hmm. Maybe." Charles paused, his coffee cup poised in front of his mouth. "Are you thinking about the poison pen campaign?"

"Well, partly," Louise acknowledged. "It didn't go the way we thought it would, but it wasn't a complete failure either. Still, I think we should try something different."

"I'm convinced," said Charles.

"Any ideas on where we should go to think about our mission?" asked Louise.

"Yes, actually." Charles set his coffee cup down on the window sill and peered out toward the woonboot, but there was nothing moving at this early hour. "I'd like to see the area where Operation Market Garden took place," he said.

"That's Arnhem, right?" Louise asked.

"Yes." He turned to face her. "Well, it ended in Arnhem. It began on the other side of the river, and there were battles in several different areas."

"Can we do it in a day?" she asked, looking at him over her coffee cup.

"A day wouldn't be enough to see everything," he said, leaning back in his chair, "but I don't want to re-enact the battle, I just want to see the bridge and some of the places where the fighting was. There should be some memorials too. I'd like to see them. Two days should do it."

"OK," she said with the finality of a decision. "The guys in the woonboot will still be here when we get back."

They rented a car from an Amsterdam dealer and drove out of the city, heading east into the countryside, which was unrelentingly flat and snow-covered. The farm fields were sliced into grazing areas by lines of straight-as-an-arrow trenches, frozen solid for the winter. The open areas were a welcome relief from the closed confines of their apartment and the daily monitoring of the woonboot. Perhaps in a different environment they could flesh out the details of the Love Campaign they had thought of. The setback from the poisoned pen letter wasn't serious. In fact it helped them re-examine the premises they'd been operating on. A new tack seemed appealing.

Farther into the countryside, Charles remarked, "Amsterdam is almost like a separate country. It has a completely cosmopolitan feeling about it—it's more like a small version of Paris or London than a Dutch town."

"It has one of the major orchestras of the world, an immensely important museum, and an airport, judged to be the best in the world," Louise offered. "Not many small towns can make those statements."

"Remember that waiter we spoke to in the restaurant on the Prinsengracht—I forget the name of the restaurant—who said that it was a mistake to think that you are seeing the Netherlands when you are in Amsterdam?" Charles said, stealing glances at her as he drove.

"Yes. I remember him—straight blond hair, balding a little, pale blue eyes, what they call a "typical" Dutch face, although it isn't very typical anymore." She paused. "So now we are going to see the real Netherlands, I guess."

"You've been reading up on it, haven't you?"

"You know me. I can't resist a good brochure."

"Did you read the word *polder* in the brochure?"

"I did, but it's just a field, isn't it?" she asked.

"It's more than that. A polder is an area that's been reclaimed from the sea," Charles explained.

"But they're still pumping," Louise protested.

"So?"

"It doesn't seem to me that they can say the land is 'reclaimed,' if they're still working on it."

Charles thought for a moment. "It does sound more final than it is. But, on the other hand, they can use it to grow crops."

"I see," Louise said.

The fragile dependency of huge farms on innocuous, nearly invisible machinery, struck Charles and Louise as a symbol of what modern Holland was all about. The economy was one of the most robust in Europe, and the country one of the richest in the world. But these riches had been won by generations of hard work and technical mastery, though Dutch modesty prevented their boasting about it. Or almost. Their pride of accomplishment wasn't far below the surface, and given an invitation, the Dutch would tell any visitor about their successes.

"It must have had some kind of impact on the national character," Charles said.

"What must have?" Louise, driving now and focused on traffic problems, was a bit sharp.

"The whole dike thing, being lower than the sea, under threat of flooding." Charles kept looking at the snow-covered fields.

"Do you mean it's made them insular?" Louise gave him a side-long glance, filled with skepticism.

"No," said Charles. "I don't think they *are* insular, really. They seem to participate in all the events of Europe and the world, although they do so rather quietly. But they have a strong sense of community, of doing things in concert." Charles admired his own idea. It was based for the most part on books he'd been reading and conversations he and Louise had had with their landlord, with waiters and others.

"Of course, any culture has a strong sense of community compared to America." Louise made this comment after driving silently for a while.

"What does that mean?" Charles asked, puzzled.

"Our American tendency to go it alone," Louise explained.

"Yes, sure, said Charles, "but that's not the opposite of community. Any small town in Kansas will admire the man who can do things on his own, who takes on the world or invents a new way, but the people there still have a strong sense of community."

"OK," Louse said, "but don't they admire creativity and spunk here? An inventor? A scientist who makes a discovery?"

"Yes, I suppose they do, but I suspect that they admire the inventor more if he shares his new idea with all his neighbors before he sends it in to the patent office."

"And you think this comes from battling the sea with dikes and pumps?" The skeptical tone had returned to Louise's voice.

"It's a little far-fetched, isn't it?" Charles allowed.

"You could say that."

"But I still think living under the threat of flooding for centuries—and they had some terrible floods—must have influenced the national consciousness."

"You would think it would make them all anxiety-ridden," Louise said, "but I don't see any evidence of that."

"How about their famous tolerance?" Charles asked.

"I don't see how that could be connected with being lower than sea level." Louise's skepticism was growing. She could see Charles digging himself into a logical hole.

"Well, maybe not so precisely," Charles said, laughing a little at the absurdity of the idea, "but they have very little patience with small-mindedness, and that's really what their tolerance is all about."

"I can see a kind of connection there," Louise allowed, and Charles smiled at the new tone of acceptance in her voice. "If you're under threat from anything, it's more than a waste of time not to connect with someone just because of some quirk or odd belief. It could be dangerous."

"Yes. I can see that part of it," Charles said, but now it was his turn to be skeptical.

"Besides, this business of national characteristics is really silly. Not every Frenchman is a lover; not every American is a businessman. *Et cetera et cetera.*" Louise stated this idea with finality.

"National characteristics could never be anything more than tendencies anyway," Charles allowed.

"Where I think they may be important," Louise amended her original idea, "is that once the belief of a characteristic is accepted by the population itself, then they may begin to feel that they *should* be that way."

"You mean the Dutch person who is feeling judgmental toward someone will try to hide it because it isn't tolerant and therefore not very Dutch?" Charles found this an interesting idea that seemed to lead to a better understanding of the Dutch, who were, he thought, often difficult to understand.

"Sure," Louise went on, "just like the American who knows he is supposed to be a rugged individualist will hesitate to ask for help because he's violating a supposition about Americans. I have seen that in psychotherapy."

"What you are saying is that the worst thing about these national cultural virtues is that we believe them ourselves," Charles concluded.

"Exactly."

They drove on in silence.

Chapter 10
The Bridge

After an hour and a half of driving on superhighways, Charles saw a sign.

"Arnhem!" he shouted, "where Market Garden ended, you know, the book *A Bridge Too Far*.'"

"Yes, I know. I think I even read it. I don't think I finished it though. Not my kind of book. Arnhem is where the famous bridge is, right?"

"Yes. Let's go take a look at it. That was one of my favorite books," he added a little petulantly.

"OK. Drive on. Drive over the bridge too far," she said.

"Before we do that, let's look at some of the towns around the outskirts where the first part of the story was set."

"OK with me."

"As I remember the story opens on the south side of the Rhine, and the Polish troops are coming in by air. The Americans and the British came up a highway linking Arnhem to Nijmegen I think it was. The Poles were dropped in by parachute and some in gliders."

Charles, talking excitedly, missed a turn, and realized in a moment that they were crossing the Rhine on a bridge.

"Is this the bridge?" Louise asked.

"No. It can't be. We aren't that close to Arnhem yet. I don't know what this bridge is. It's too new to be the one in the book."

As soon as they were on the other side they got off the highway to look at the map. They were in a town called Heteren, on the south side of the Rhine, not much more than a main street of shops and restaurants surrounded by groups of houses, connected one with the other as most Dutch houses were. The houses were farther away from the center of town, and beyond the houses were the wide, snowy fields of the dairy farms. The cattle, however, were huddled in the barns keeping warm.

"It's a very cute town," said Louise. "Let's have lunch here."

"Suits me. I am getting hungry."

A sign on an otherwise simple building said *"De koffie is klaar."*

"It just means they're open for business," Charles explained.

"But why should the coffee be clear anyway? It sounds watery and awful." Louise was teasing Charles, but he didn't catch on, and she knew that a seriously linguistic explanation would follow.

"'Klaar' means 'ready.' The coffee is ready. It's supposed to be welcoming."

"I get it."

They went in. The restaurant was small, with a dozen tables covered with checkered tablecloths. Small wooden chairs were arranged neatly around each table. The room was warm, thankfully, and they hung their winter coats and hats on a nearby coat rack, a series of little hooks with numbers painted on each one. Charles, hanging up the coats, puzzled over the numbers. They seemed unnecessary. A long display case stood at one side, showing various snacks. A smiling waitress with auburn hair and dark eyes—not the typical Dutch face, which, they were learning, was somewhat rare—greeted them in English, and gave them menus, then walked back behind the counter.

"Why did she speak English?" Louise whispered. "Is it so obvious that we're Americans?"

"No, I don't think so, but it's obvious that we're travelers and not Dutch, so English seems the best choice."

"It's the clothes, I think," said Charles. "They don't look Dutch. I can't tell you why, specifically."

When she came back to their table to take their order, however, Charles spoke to her in Dutch, and he took it as confirmation that his accent was good when she answered him in Dutch. He knew that if he showed even the trace of an accent, the people would speak to him in English, both because it was an opportunity for them to practice their second language and because it seemed polite to speak in a language more familiar to strangers than Dutch.

"You must have Dutch parents," the waitress said.

"Exactly," Charles lied. It was the simplest explanation. "May I ask you a question?"

"Certainly."

"Why do the coat hooks have numbers on them?"

"Ah, yes, I am sure that looks odd. You see, they were tearing down an old school not far from here, and the neighbors were invited to come in and take whatever appealed to them. These are the hooks that the children hung their coats on. Each child had a number."

"I see. They're a little memory of the past."

"I guess they are. But in the new school the hooks have numbers too." She paused for a moment. "But the new numbers are very clinical looking, not like these."

Charles looked again, and realized that indeed the numbers under the hooks had a Germanic flavor to them, just as he had seen in older Dutch texts. Today, all typefaces were resolutely simple and American looking.

They ordered a plate of little sandwiches—a small amount of ham and cheese on a little roll—and some of the famous *"klaar"* coffee. They used these times to consider and reconsider their missions, and since their trip today was for stock-taking, they began without introduction.

"I think we're doing what the President asked," Louise said. "Of course, the poisoned pen letter was a mistake, but otherwise I think we are on target."

"Yes, we're slowing them down and sowing dissension," Charles allowed, leaning forward on his elbows. "But what do we do next?" As usual, he answered his own question. "We can't keep doing the same things over and over. They'll catch on. Whatever we do has to look like bad luck."

"Or an angry God," Charles added as an afterthought.

"Yes. That was a good idea," Louise said with some admiration. "Should we do it with one of the others?"

"Maybe," said Charles. "But it'll have to be different somehow. They might compare notes, and that would blow the whole thing wide open. A different medium, maybe, or a different message."

"I thought the medium was the message." Louise's eyes glinted as she made a small joke.

"In this case there is some truth to that," Chares said rocking back in his chair, then concluded, "I think it would be best not to try the God thing again. It's too risky."

"What about some other dirty tricks?" Louise offered.

"There is the woonboot," said Charles. "It's certainly vulnerable. I think a slow leak would mess them up. They'd have to have the woonboot hauled out and repaired."

"Wouldn't they just move out and let it sink?" Louise countered. "They're just renting." She'd lived in New York City and understood the renter's mentality.

"I don't think so. I'm sure they're trying to be on good behavior. They don't want to get in trouble with the law. Remember the discussion they had after the bank incident; that really challenged them. If they tried to desert the woonboot as it sank, the landlord could find them through bank records. Everybody uses the system for paying bills. The accounts are private, but the police can get a warrant for the address of someone who's not paying rent. I don't think they'd risk getting in trouble with the law. Not a second time."

"So they'd have to repair it?" Louise asked.

"No. The owner would have to repair it, but it would disrupt their lives. I think they'd have to live in a hotel for a few weeks while their quarters were being repaired."

"That would inconvenience us as much as them," Louise noted.

"That's a good point. If we can find something to do that lets us keep our current setup it would certainly be better."

"But, suppose we do it. How would we make the woonboot develop a slow leak?" Louise was quite curious, and her face was twisted into a shape that showed it. She couldn't imagine what they might do, given the public nature of the woonboot.

"I don't know, Charles said, shaking his head. Maybe Henderson can get us some technical help for that."

"The food supply is still vulnerable. We could do something again with that," Louise suggested.

"Yes. But something different. I would like it if we could target just one of them. And let's not give them diarrhea again."

"OK. We could inject one piece of fruit with a drug. A light dose of LSD maybe. It will make the one who gets it look crazy to the others."

"Can we protect the Kuwaiti?"

"Sure. We can have Henderson talk to the guy who's running him. Tell him not to eat any fruit."

"That should work."

"That's two ideas."

"Plus the God thing, which is already there. It cranks it all up a notch in intensity and we don't have to do anything more about it."

"OK."

Lunch came. It was simple fare but good, and they ate it in silence, Louise thinking about other possibilities for messing with the cell, Charles about the ways their new plans could go wrong and what they could do to guard against them.

Chapter 11
The Village

After lunch, they drove back toward the bridge, but as they approached it, they saw another road, up on top of the dike, and they decided to drive along it just to see what there was on this side of the river. There were surely some other small villages, and the farmland looked pretty.

There was a layer of new snow on the fields, and the sheep and cattle were all in the sheds, their bodies generating heat.

"I read that in the old days, said Louise, "the farmers kept the animals in the house they lived in and used their body heat to conserve heating fuel."

"It must have smelled pretty awful, said Charles, imagining the onslaught to his sensitive nose.

"And there would have been a lot of infection from fecal-borne bacteria," Louise added.

They came to the village of Driel, which Charles immediately recognized as the opening scene of *A Bridge Too Far*. Driving along the main street, they saw houses that had been given Polish names, and in the main square a statue honored the Polish general, Sosabowski, whose troops landed in the town in gliders and by parachute.

"This was the first action of the battle," said Charles. "Many of the Poles were killed by German fire as they drifted down, helpless in their parachute harnesses. Others were shot in their gliders as soon as they landed. It was a slaughter of the Polish troops."

As they rode around the town, Charles recognized on some of the farm buildings and mailboxes the names of local Dutch families who had figured in the story of the invasion.

The recent snow made the roads too slippery for bicycles, even for the highly-skilled Dutch bikers, and people hurried along the street, hunched against the cold. A few seemed to be enjoying the cold, walking more slowly, stopping to talk with their neighbors in small groups, their breath steaming.

Two churches soared above the town. The first was directly in front of the road that came down off the dike. It looked very old to the two Americans, so they stopped and read the sign on the front door.

"1400," Louise exclaimed. "It's been very well cared for, though, hasn't it?"

Charles tried the door and found it open. They stepped inside.

"It's so clean," Charles said. "It looks as though it was dusted less than an hour ago."

The wooden pews gleamed in the light slanting in from the high windows on the dike side. Beyond the pews, straightbacked and tall, rose an elaborate structure, carved with rococo abandon in an exotic dark wood.

"What is that?" Louise asked pointing at the structure that dominated the space.

"It's the *preekstoel*," Charles said. "The preacher had to climb up those stairs—look how elaborately they're carved—two flights of them, to get to the pulpit where he could look down at his flock."

"Hmm," Louise hummed, her sense of rebellion at authoritarianism barely concealed.

Back outside, they found a small cemetery, with several rows of old stones and markers, meticulously cared for, with growing flowers and cut grass.

Louise pointed silently at a newly dug grave.

"Maybe a town official," Charles suggested.

"Why do you think that?" Louise asked.

"The churchyard space is so small, not big enough for just anyone to be buried here," he said.

They returned to their car and drove farther down the main street. A few hundred yards farther on, they found the newer Roman Catholic church. The churches faced each other at either end of the town's main street.

"It's like they're facing off, like hockey players before the puck is tossed, waiting for the next soul to be battled over," Charles said.

"I didn't think the Dutch were so religious," Louise said.

"Well, they aren't any more," Charles said, "but before World War II there was fierce sectarian differences. The Catholic and Protestant elements of society were so often viciously at each other's throats that the government was forced to separate them into pillars."

"Pillars?" Louise asked quizzically.

"Everything was divided according to religion. There were different hospitals to be born in, different towns to grow up in, different schools, different stores and business, and in the end different hospitals to die in and different churchyards to be buried in."

"So they didn't need to encounter people of a different persuasion," Louise commented. "What an extreme solution."

"I suppose so," Charles said, "but it worked well enough until World War II shattered all the old ways, and damaged the deep religiosity of the nation. After the war, and the horrible hunger that the Germans imposed on their rebellious "little Aryan brothers," the Netherlands became supremely secular, and the need for the pillars melted slowly away."

"But if these 'pillars' separated the whole country into Catholic and Protestant towns, why are there two churches here in Driel?" Louise asked.

"I don't know," Charles said. "But this town is in the middle of the country, neither the protestant north or the catholic south.

I suppose they had to learn to tolerate each other, but it couldn't have been easy."

"I'm sure no one wanted their daughter to marry one, whichever of the two the 'one' was," Louise commented.

They looked again, and with somewhat different eyes, at the groups of villagers, bundled up against the cold, and blowing the steam of Netherlandic breath in each others' faces. Bucolic and charming as the town was, they had exhausted its possibilities in an hour and got back on the dike, heading toward Arnhem. From the elevated dike, they looked out on the Rhine, low this time of year, but still deep enough to float a series of riverboats and small barges, carrying goods from Germany to the cities of the coast. The riverboats often had the owner's little car parked on an afterdeck, and the day's laundry flying stiffly in the cold wind, while children played on a middle deck, bundled up in scarves and woolen hats.

"Someday," said Louise, "I would like to travel on one of those riverboats through Europe, preferably in warmer weather. It looks comfortable, relaxing, and romantic."

"I think there is a growing tourist trade in riverboat tours," said Charles.

"But the dikes make it difficult to see into the villages, at least here in the Netherlands," she thought.

"And that's a shame because those cute little cottages are one of the beautiful sights of the country," said Charles. "But look, there's a house, standing by itself, on the river side of the dike."

"It's got the pulled-back lace curtains like they all do."

"And see the flower boxes framing the doors and windows. They're waiting for spring."

There was ice on the river, but the riverboats were chugging right through it, sending cakes of it—about four inches thick they estimated—cascading off the boats' sides with a wash of river water, then sliding like hockey pucks for long distances on the surface toward the banks.

"In a few more weeks, if the weather stays cold, the rivers will freeze solid," said Charles, "and all the boat traffic will stop, and the skaters will come out."

"Do you know about the Eleven Cities Tour?" Louise asked as they drove along the dike.

"It's a skating race, isn't it?"

"I don't think it's actually a race. More like a tour or rally, but when the winter is particularly cold, a lot of people skate each day to another city, using the rivers and canals as roadways, until they have completed a big circle over much of the country and have visited eleven cities. All along the way, the locals turn out, lining the canals and rivers to cheer them on."

"It sounds like fun," said Charles, "both the skating and the watching."

"They drink a lot of beer then," added Louise, "which surely contributes to the fun."

They drove along the dike until they came to a railroad bridge.

"That must be the bridge that was dynamited and left hanging in the river," Charles said, excited to find a place described in the book.

"Or, maybe, it's a new one in the same place." Louise's sarcasm was evident, but it did nothing to quell Charles' enthusiasm. Ahead, he could see the twin towers of the cathedral at Arnhem, which had survived the battle. He pointed it out to Louise.

"It looks lopsided," she said.

"I think there was a lot of damage, and one of the towers was damaged to the point that it was shorter than the other one. From this distance, the church looks lopsided. But at least it didn't fall."

They came then to the next bridge, a new one, which Charles disdained—it was obviously built after the war—and a little farther on the famous "bridge too far" over which so many German and American and British soldiers, and not a few Dutch citizens, had died in the battle that lasted for days, ending in a defeat for the allies and a painful withdrawal, first to the west, then back over the river they had crossed weeks earlier, carrying their wounded. Many Americans and Englishmen died in an operation that was poorly conceived. They drove over the bridge and Charles could see, now restored, the very same houses that had figured prominently in the short, violent history of the battle for the town.

Once in the city, they found a parking lot and left the car, preferring to walk. From the parking lot, a shopping area could be seen, closed off to automobile traffic.

Arnhem had a pleasantly active quality, people bustling about but not impeded by too many other shoppers. There were only a few main streets in the primary shopping area, three of them stretching back from the market, which was in front of the cathedral, to the more central part of the city, where the train station, banks, and municipal buildings were located. In short, it was big enough to have whatever a person might want to buy, but small enough to get around in.

Charles found a music store, filled with classical sheet music, and bought enough flute solo books to keep him happy for several years. Louise found antique stores, jewelry stores, and a shop with a large selection of many things for the kitchen. She bought several bags full.

By the time they were done shopping, they were hungry. On one of the main streets they found a kind of restaurant, half open to the street even in December, selling French fries in paper cones, like British fish and chips but cleaner, and a huge assortment of sauces to put over them, from mayonnaise, which was the preferred covering in this country, to Thai satay sauce, rich with garlic, tomato, and peanuts. They did also have catsup, but why, the American couple figured, go to a foreign country and eat the way you do at home? Charles ordered satay sauce, and Louise a kind of meat gravy. They took their little cones and two cups of hot Dutch coffee to a small table in the back, away from the cold air, and sat down.

They finished their fries and went back for more, Louise now trying the satay sauce and Charles a sweet and sour sauce. They both pronounced the satay the best, although Louise said the meat gravy wasn't bad. But the sweet and sour was awful over French fries. Sipping their coffee to top off their satisfied appetites, they thought again about their mission.

"I've been thinking that the slow leak isn't such a good idea," Louise said.

"Why?"

Well, first, I can't see how we can do it without getting caught," she said. "Now that it's gotten colder, there are people skating by all the time, even at night, so we can't suddenly kneel down and drill a hole. We can't chop through the ice to attach a little explosive charge or an acid corrosive. I don't think we want to hire a sharp-shooter to put a bullet just below the waterline."

"Definitely not," Charles said. "I was hoping that Henderson's colleagues would find a technical solution."

"Well, maybe they will, but I bet not."

"And second?"

"Second," said Louise, "is that if they have to take the woonboot to a repair facility and live in a hotel for a few weeks it's going to disrupt our lives just as much as theirs and make our job harder."

"These are convincing arguments."

"Thank you."

"So, we have the touch of LSD," Charles said, "which I think we should go forward with. It will create dissension among them."

"OK." Louise was already thinking of another idea. "It may not be much, but maybe we could find some way to help one of these guys fall in love."

"Yes, the love campaign." It's an interesting idea; it creates an outside interest, a strong pull away from the cell. It might even thwart their plans. But how can we make it happen?" Charles leaned forward, his brow furrowed.

"We can't make it happen," she agreed, "but we can create the right conditions for it—plow the soil, fertilize, plant the seed. Then, we will have to let the garden grow through human nature, hormones, and youth," Louise said with a wide smile.

"Maybe that Jordanian girl who called Akhmed," said Charles.

"Have you gotten a look at her?" Louise was considering the constraints under which hormones and youth operate.

"No. I've only been to the school once," admitted Charles.

"Well, let's pay a visit to the school then," said Louise.

They bussed the remains of their snack to a trash can like dutiful Americans used to the rules of fast food dining, picked up their packages, and re-entered the Arnhem street scene. But the shopping had become tiresome and the passing crowd less interesting. They were glad to get back to their car, figure out the strange method for paying the parking lot fee, and leave Arnhem. In fact, they were eager to get back to their "work," which now had more appeal than before.

Chapter 12
The Love Campaign

On the drove back to Amsterdam, ways to "assist" two people in the process of falling in love drifted in and out of their minds. If it happened, it could drive a wedge between the lover and the other cell members. Back in their apartment by eleven, Louise turned on the equipment while Charles looked out the window at the woonboot. Everything seemed quiet. Listening on the "intercom," as they'd come to call it, only the television could be heard. They turned everything off, fell into bed and slept soundly.

The usual morning routine—listening to a recording of the previous day's conversations, skipping quickly over the many uninteresting parts while sipping morning coffee and eating toast and jam -- occupied an hour. At ten, they took the train for a first look at the university.

The Free University of Amsterdam was like urban universities in the States—just another group of buildings in the city. There was no quadrangle, no lawns on which students could lounge and talk or play Frisbee. Lounging, which was not frequent among the always busy Dutch, was done upright in groups in the hallways. For more serious lounging, the kind that required sitting down, the students went to the cafeteria, which was below ground level and sat at tables, drinking coffee or beer and engaging in the endless discussions that twenty-somethings use to sharpen their worldviews.

Louise had quickly oriented herself to the various buildings and offices. Charles still had to read the signs. They did, however, find the room where Akhmed, Osama, and Arthur were taking a course in Dutch history. As a cover, in case anyone challenged their presence, they found a nameplate on the third floor identifying one Professor van Oeveren and if anyone asked who they were, they would say they were trying to find him. But, as in many universities, the application of the rules was casual, and no one asked.

Students trickled in to the lecture hall. When the two Arabs and the American arrived, Charles and Louise paid close attention to the people they spoke to. One Arabic-looking girl seemed particularly interested in Akhmed. She was, they were pleased to see, dressed more in the Dutch fashion than in conservative Muslim attire, and she did not cover her face with a scarf. She was pretty enough, and they hoped it was the same girl who'd called during the plague of intestinal sickness. The woonboot's telephone records would show the name and number of the girl who'd called, but was it the same one who seemed now to be engaging Akhmed's attention?

More importantly, Charles noted, it wasn't clear what they were going to do. Forcing two young people together could easily backfire. From their own youth they remembered that forced meetings create awkwardness and resistance, but chance encounters, or ones that looked like chance, might work. They just needed to create conditions in which the young people ran into each other and had an opportunity to talk.

An approaching concert by a popular Dutch folk singer offered an opportunity. An American rock concert, of which there were plenty, would have been too loud and too politically loaded. There was also the possibility, actually a certainty here in Amsterdam, that a rock concert would include heavy marijuana use, which would dampen their efforts. The folk concert seemed about right, but did the two people have any interest in folk music? From a ticket seller at a kiosk in the street they bought two tickets in adjacent seats before boarding the train and heading back to their apartment.

Examining the records of incoming phone calls during the "Diarrhea Days" they found the call from a girl identifying herself as Takhmina. With the number they found her full name—Takhmina Konets—and her address in a student housing area not far from the university.

The finally devised plan was to send a ticket to each of them with a cover letter from a local radio station specializing in folk music and light rock, saying that the two had been selected at random to get the enclosed tickets. Louise was eager to administer the "touch of LSD" plot, but Charles pointed out that there was no way to control which terrorist got the dose. If it should turn out to be Akhmed who got the drug, it would crimp—probably destroy—any developing relationship with Takhmina. So the "touch of LSD" plot had to go first.

From earlier inspections of their garbage, Charles knew they were fond of fresh oranges, and by injecting a small amount of the drug into one orange they were almost certain to dose only one of the terrorists. The idea was to make it look as though one of them had lost his mind. But they didn't want him to be taken to a hospital, where he would surely be tested. The presence of a drug would tip the terrorists off that someone was harassing them. So they planned on blocking their cell phone transmissions as soon as they knew the drug was working. As a further precaution, they would disable their car at the same time. Timing would be crucial.

On the next Monday, when Muhammad returned from a shopping trip, Charles and Louise once again opened the trunk of the terrorists' car while it was left unlocked during the unloading of groceries, but they found no oranges, and no other item seemed so perfect for injecting a small fluid. The oranges must have gone in with the first load. So they were forced to wait another week. But then, on the following Monday, they found a bag of oranges and injected a very small dose of LSD into one, closed the trunk and walk away with feigned indifference.

Chapter 13
The Dose

From the apartment, Louise continued to monitor all phone calls in real time, and on Wednesday morning she heard a call to a hospital emergency room.

"My cousin, he acts very strangely. He…"

Louise shut the call down. At the same time, Charles hurried out to the street to let the air out of at least one tire. He had just finished when he heard the hatch opening and loud voices in Arabic trying to get Osama, for it was he who had eaten the dosed orange, up the stairs and across the inner woonboot to the car. Charles walked away toward the train station like a man late for work. He didn't look back, but he was listening very carefully to what was happening behind him.

Osama was calling out loudly, "There are little birds everywhere! They keep flying in my face! Let me go! Look out!"

He wanted his arms free so that he could swat at the imaginary little birds, but Akhmed and Muhammad were propelling him toward the car.

"Take it easy! There are no birds!"

It was a struggle, but they finally got him in the car. He calmed down a little, swatting only occasionally. When they tried to drive away, the car pulled strongly to one side, and they had to pull over before they had even left the block. Their right front tire was flat. Charles, walking in the other direction, was far enough away to stop and look back at the scene. They walked Osama back toward the woonboot. He was calming more and more, making only an occasional swat in front of his face. So they got him back down the hatch. Finding himself in the same environment brought the hallucinations back for several minutes, and both brothers had to restrain him again. Charles went back up to the apartment, where Louise was already listening on the "intercom." Eventually, Osama calmed down and stopped swatting, and for about 15 minutes he sat silently while the rest of the cell members stared at him, ready to pin him down if necessary. Then he giggled. If he had laughed in a way that suggested it was all a joke, they could have handled it, but he giggled like a schoolgirl. They kept watching him. He kept giggling.

"Stop that!" Akhmed yelled.

More giggling.

"Stop it!"

More giggling, but quieter.

"Just sit still for a while. Allah watches you," said Ibrahim.

The other brothers looked at Ibrahim. He had become more religious since they'd all been sick, making references to Allah or quoting scripture. They weren't sure what to make of him. Now this weird thing with Osama was an additional problem and Ibrahim's reaction to it seemed impractical and off base.

Osama had stopped giggling. Everyone stared at him, wondering what he would do next.

"Can I go to sleep?" he asked.

"Sure," said Akhmed. And he got up and walked Osama back to his bed, where he lay down and began snoring. Akhmed came back to the kitchen where they were all sitting. "Well, what should we do?"

"Let's just let him sleep and see what he's like when he wakes up," offered Talgat, the Kuwaiti.

"I will pray for guidance," suggested Ibrahim.

"Yeah, let him sleep it off," said Arthur/Anwar.

This caused Talgat, the mole, to look at Anwar. Maybe Anwar suspected that Osama had been drugged. The others, Talgat was sure, thought Osama had lost his marbles. And he was right. The other two brothers were worried about him, and

Ibrahim was pretty sure that it was another visitation from God. If his cell phone were to ring at this moment, he would have answered with resignation and obedience in his voice. But it didn't.

Arthur, who had dropped some acid in his earlier days, recognized the symptoms and figured that Osama had succumbed to one of the many pleasures Amsterdam had to offer. If he'd been a little smarter he would have realized that it was not in Osama's character to take such a step. The Kuwaiti mole still had his fingers crossed, but was beginning to feel hopeful that the latest attempt to screw them over was going to interfere with their operation without making them suspicious. This was the substance of his report to his handler later that afternoon, and the same report was forwarded to Henderson.

Chapter 14
The Tickets

So, having sown dissension in one way, Charles and Louise set to work on the second, sending the concert tickets off to Takhmina and Akhmed. In a day or two, Akhmed received his surprise in the mail. He had no particular interest in Dutch folk music, but it was a free ticket, and he didn't see any reason not to go, as he would have if it had been an American rock concert. Ibrahim advised him not to go, muttering something about Allah and western music, and within himself fully suspicious of the source of the free tickets. Akhmed had gone back to drinking and whoring after recovering from his sickness. But Ibrahim was not strenuous in his objections; Dutch folk music was pretty bland, and much of it was anti-American. Muhammad was simply jealous; he would like to have gone himself. Arthur/Anwar was contemptuous of all of them.

So it was with an unencumbered conscience that Akhmed found his seat in the concert hall and was surprised when Takhmina came and sat down next to him.

She was not the girl that Charles and Louise had seen Akhmed speak to in the lecture hall, but she was Arabic. She was much prettier than the other girl, and she was dressed appropriately for a folk concert in tight, faded jeans, which showed off her splendid figure, and a festive winter sweater. Akhmed too had dressed in as western a style as his wardrobe permitted. So, at least as far as clothes—and the statement they make—were concerned, the two were meeting on common ground.

"Oh, hi, you're…"

"Takhmina, from the university. What are you doing here?"

"I, for, I am coming to the concert." Akhmed switched from Dutch to Arabic, stumbling in his confusion. "They sent me a free ticket."

"Ah, me too." She had the cover letter that Louise had composed with her and took it out to show him.

"Yes. That's the same that I got."

They had no real reason to be suspicious. Anyone giving away free tickets would probably buy them in a block, and university students were a prime target audience for a radio station that broadcast folk music. Their seating next to each other was not at all improbable.

They chatted while waiting for the curtain to go up. She was from Jordan, he from Saudi Arabia, which made both of them a little suspicious of each other for political reasons—they were in fact on opposite sides of the political spectrum—but for politeness and because they were young, single, attractive, and sitting next to each other, both moderated their views. In any case, they had a common anti-Americanism to fall back on.

"What are you majoring in?" Akhmed asked while they waited for the concert to begin.

"I am premed; I am going to become a doctor," she said simply. It was a simple statement, but there was much information in it. Arabic women in most countries did not seek education, and in many countries they were forbidden to educate themselves. To go to the university was itself a step that broke from a girl's family, country, and religion, but to go on beyond that and prepare oneself for a profession was quite extraordinary. "What are you studying?"

"I am studying business. I like it very much." Of course, he could not tell her the true reason for his being in the Netherlands. He was intrigued, even fascinated, by her ambition to become a doctor. A whole world of possibility opened up to him just from hearing her plans. She may have been a little smarter than he was, but that was OK. He didn't want to become a doctor. But if she could become a doctor, or even just make the attempt, then he could make an attempt too, at business perhaps. He was doing pretty well in his English classes, and business had always appealed to him. So he asked her question after question about her plans.

"Where will you get the money?"

"My parents are paying for my education."

"Where will you go to medical school? Here?"

"Yes, I think so. They have good medical schools here. They are based on the American model." Somehow, she conveyed her distaste for America while at the same time showing her preference for the American form of medical education.

"How long will it take you to become a doctor?" Akhmed asked.

"Probably four years after the university, but it depends on what I specialize in." She had almost decided to specialize in obstetrics and gynecology, knowing the terrible state of women's diseases and the occasional horror of childbirth gone wrong in her homeland, but she was still an Arab girl and could not mention such a thing to a boy.

"Do you want to practice here in the Netherlands?" Akhmed asked.

"No I don't think so. But maybe. I don't know. It is also possible that I will go back to Jordan. But," she turned to him and smiled in a way that made him stop breathing for a moment. "I spent a wonderful week in Denmark last year. It is a beautiful country. And they love children." The smile again, softer now. Akhmed's heart skipped a beat. Then she went on. "I was in Sweden once too and it is very beautiful, but I think Denmark is a little bit more fun."

The more she talked the more his heart opened up to a better plan for himself than martyrdom. He was too young to die, or rot in a Dutch prison. And the more his heart opened to these possibilities, the more it opened also to her, the angel who brought the glad tidings.

As for her, she enjoyed talking to the young Saudi. He was attractive, she thought, if a little intense for her taste, but he was very attentive and interested in her, which was an improvement over the other men she had met in her premed classes. They seemed to talk only about themselves, what they would specialize in, where they would go to medical school and how much money they would make. After talking to a few of them, she found them boring.

Then the curtain went up, and they sat back and enjoyed the concert far more than they would have if they hadn't met. They exchanged cell phone numbers afterwards. Giving her number to him, and writing his down, let him know that she would like to talk to him again. They parted company outside the concert hall, smiling and shaking hands, and Akhmed walked home with lighter footsteps than he could remember since coming to the Netherlands. "In fact," he thought, "I haven't felt this good since I was a boy."

Takhmina also had a pleasant trip back to her apartment. She saw some possibilities. Maybe there could be a relationship. She wasn't sure. Her steps were not lighter, indeed, Takhmina's feet were always firmly on the ground, but she could see how, if things worked out in the right way, that she could practice medicine in Europe while married to a fine Muslim man who ran a successful international business.

Neither of them could remember anything at all about the concert.

Louise and Charles did not know any of this. But when a call went out from Akhmed to Takhmina three days later, asking her to meet him for coffee after class, they smiled at each other, and if they had been 15 or 20 years younger would have high-fived each other. If they had to do dirty tricks, this was much more fun than giving everyone diarrhea.

Chapter 15
The Dossier

In the woonboot, things were not going well. Arthur/Anwar was particularly bothered by the changes. He sensed that they were falling apart. Akhmed seemed distracted, often staring off into space. Ibrahim spent more time at the mosque than he used to, and every day he read the Holy Qur'an. Osama was getting better, but he was not exactly right either. Every once in a while, usually at breakfast, he would swat something away from his face, or giggle for no apparent reason. Muhammad seemed OK, but he was worried about his brothers and his cousin.

"Arthur is the only remaining strong-willed force in the terrorist cell," Louise said, as they sipped coffee and ate really good Dutch bread, toasted, with jam and butter, for breakfast.

"Ibrahim needs a little more prodding too," she went on. Muhammad has always been weak and will simply follow his brothers if they give up."

"Let's see if Henderson has any more information on Arthur," Charles suggested. "They probably have a large dossier on him. He is an American traitor, after all."

Louise went to her computer and began massaging the keyboard.

In a day, a substantial dossier came back by diplomatic pouch to the U.S. Embassy in Amsterdam. They picked it up, took it back to their apartment and read it carefully. It was remarkably detailed. Dossiers assembled on individuals that are suspected of subversive activities are typically as comprehensive as possible, but Arthur's background was particularly interesting to the authorities. He was not only an American who'd joined a terrorist organization, but also a white, middle-class youth from a liberal state. So the dossier was developed out of interviews with many who knew Arthur well, and some who knew him less well, but had some unusual insight into his behavior. Louise read the massive document with astonishment.

Arthur had been raised in Sacramento, an only child. Looking at the clinical descriptions of Arthur's background, Louise had no difficulty reading between the lines. His parents, powerfully distracted by their own careers and ambitions, paid no more attention to him than was necessary. He was adequately fed and housed, helped with his homework, and driven to soccer games, but both of the parents were always wishing they were doing something else, working on their own plans. There was little affection in the house either. The parents had been more attracted to each other's future plans than to the person they were at present, which made them both always somewhat disappointed in the other, and when Arthur came along, an accident following a rowdy New Year's Eve party, he did not make it any easier for them to reach their goals. So, although they did their best to hide it from him, there was an undercurrent of resentment in all their dealings with him. When he became a teenager, this resentment was reciprocated with an intensity that surprised all three of them.

He drank and did drugs for a while with high school friends, but he was socially awkward, not particularly appealing, somewhat scrawny, and he was not well-liked by his peers. So, the drugs and alcohol did not work to increase a sense of belonging, which he craved perhaps even more than other teenagers, and eventually he gave up both the stimulants and the search for friends. But he wanted, more desperately than before, to feel attached to something, and one day he wandered into a local mosque.

He was welcomed but not gushed at or fussed over, which would have turned him away. The people he met in the mosque had an intensity about them which matched his own and was appealing to him. He could see too that their faith gave them something in common, something that attached them to each other but also to a higher power. In short he found brothers and sisters and a father all under the same roof, and he began to study the Holy Qur'an. In the holy book he found words to live by, rules, structure, advice, practical suggestions, and here and there some inspiring poetry. The anger against infidels also appealed to him.

During the time of his Qur'anic studies, he met a young woman, slightly older than himself. She lived with her parents, who were observant Muslims, and she was herself careful to live by the laws and customs of her religion, but for her the practice of Islam was simply a part of who she was, a part she simply accepted in the same way she accepted her thick, tumbling black hair, which she kept hidden from the eyes of men, or her tall statuesque good looks. For Arthur, however, she became something like a Saint—an embodiment of his newfound family and faith.

He could not have said whether he was more in love with her or with the idea of her, but in love he was, and he did everything he could think of to win her attention and did it with the same intensity he brought to everything. She was at first amused, and during this early phase in their relationship may have encouraged him more than she should have. He didn't need much encouragement, and the little she offered was more than enough. He was inflamed with passion for the beautiful Muslim girl. But soon, he began to seem too young, too on fire both in his ardor for her and in his attachment to Islam, which led him to frequent Koranic quotations and pronouncements, which she found tedious. In addition, he had read about, and been impressed by, the Qur'an's description of the role of the man in a Muslim family—the strong leader to whom deference and respect were paid by the women in the family. He tried to act this role in his relations with the young woman, but he had no experience with it, had certainly not seen it in his own family, and hadn't seen enough of it in the Muslim families he knew. As a result, he did not bring it off, and his attempts at it made him look foolish, if not pitiful. She began to laugh at him during these moments, which made him angry and deeply frustrated.

Soon they broke up, but he was left with the feeling that he had failed in his new faith, that he wasn't good enough, a feeling that echoed early feelings with his family and with his high school friends. But this time, it was a little different. This time he wasn't good enough as a Muslim. So, when a recruiter for Al Qaeda came to the mosque quietly looking around, talking to young people, he found in Arthur, now Anwar, fertile ground in which to sow the seeds of radicalism, violence, and martyrdom.

Charles and Louise were discouraged by what they read in the dossier.

"How can we crack that?" Charles asked.

"It's like a fortress of belief and conviction, isn't it?" Louise agreed

A few days went by.

"I've been thinking about Arthur," said Louise one morning, as they sat over coffee and pastries in a small café near the university.

"Do you have a plan for turning him?"

"No. Definitely not a plan. Just an idea."

"What is it?" Charles asked, biting into his pastry.

"That he's still a little boy emotionally. He wants his Mommy. He never really had her." She sipped her coffee.

Charles swallowed. "And what about the girl? He didn't seem to be looking for his mommy when he was interested in her."

"No. That was something else. Trying to be someone he wasn't. Also, sexual interest, I imagine." She put her coffee cup down slowly, still thinking over her idea.

"So, do you think we can find him a mommy?"

"I don't know. Could we hire someone, an actress perhaps? We've done that before."

"Mmmm. Not exactly for the same purpose." Charles was more than a little hesitant.

"No, but similar."

"It's a possibility, I guess. There's you, of course." Charles looked directly at Louise, wondering why she hadn't thought of it first.

"Yes, I've thought about that. I could do it, but I'm not sure it is a good idea. I have a lot of other things to do on this job."

"You think it would take too much time?"

"Maybe. I need to think about it. Also, we have to figure out a way to make it begin."

"Mmmm. It's not as easy as making a young couple fall in love, is it?"

"No."

They stared at the people passing by the window for a while, trying to imagine ways of introducing a mother figure into Arthur's current life. An American would probably work best, but they would have to penetrate some heavy defensive mechanisms, constructed specifically to prevent the development of any attachment, and the hurt he imagined it would cost him.

Chapter 16

The Mother

They began to follow Arthur around to get a better sense of his daily routine. They discovered quickly that he had a regular routine. After his morning classes, he went to a particular café and bought his lunch, usually the same thing, and ate it alone, reading schoolbooks or his pocket copy of the Holy Qur'an.

"Would his lunch be a good time to approach him?" Charles asked.

"I think so. I don't see why not." Louise said. "I think I see a way."

"Good. I am happy to hear it. I didn't like the actress idea. It would have been too complicated."

"And a little risky too, involving a third party."

"Right."

As she often did, Louise relied on her own instincts. She was careful to dress herself for the role she was going to play— jeans and a sweatshirt with her hair pulled back, casual, an easygoing, middle-aged American woman.

Charles fixed a "wire" under her sweatshirt, so that he could monitor the exchange, not for security—it didn't seem likely that anything could go wrong in a way that would jeopardize Louise's safety—but to save the time of Louise having to describe everything to him later. He found a spot in the café where he could watch Louise and Arthur and dawdled over a cup of coffee while reading a paperback. Louise was at another table, waiting for Arthur to come in during his lunch break. He came in, right on schedule, ordered a sandwich and a drink and found an empty table. Louise waited until he had finished the sandwich, then walked up to his table.

"You're an American, aren't you?" she said.

"Well, yes." Arthur liked forthrightness, but he did not like admitting that he was an American.

"Me too. I'm sorry to bother you. Um, may I sit down?" She put her hand on the back of the chair.

"Oh, sure, I guess so." He did not want her to sit down; he wanted to be left alone, but there seemed to be no stopping her.

"I've been trying to find decaffeinated coffee for the last hour. They don't seem to have it here. You don't know of any places, do you?"

"Um, no, I don't."

"I need it. I really like coffee, but I have trouble sleeping when I drink it. What are you doing here? Vacation?" Louise adopted a breezy manner, which she guessed would appeal to him. A waiter appeared and she ordered plain hot water.

"No, not really. I'm studying Dutch history." Arthur happened at the moment to be reading in his text on Dutch history.

"Now, why would you want to know that?"

"It's not so much that I want to. They require it."

"They? Who's they?" Her brow wrinkled.

"The Dutch government." He was still not looking at her for more than a few seconds.

"Whatever for?"

"I want to become a Dutch citizen," he said, looking straight at her with defiance. Arthur was confident that this statement would appall and repel her, as it would most patriotic Americans, so he was surprised and pleased by her reaction.

"No kidding. That's interesting. I might want to look into that. What's involved?" She leaned forward in her chair.

"Well, you have to learn to speak Dutch. That's the hardest part for me. And there's this course in the history of the Netherlands. There's a culture thing too—holidays, customs, stuff like that."

"That doesn't sound too hard. And I could learn Dutch, I think. I should check this out. I like it here. Better than the U.S. I think."

"Why do you say that?" He was interested in her take on the U.S.

"A lot of reasons. The endless series of horrible wars. Like we think we should rule the world. The President's arrogance. And not just the President—all the politicians. It doesn't matter what party they're in. They're all corrupt. I'm still embarrassed to tell people I'm an American." She paused, then went on. "I'm sorry if that's offensive. I get upset just thinking about it."

"I know what you mean. We keep invading countries. They don't deserve it."

"Certainly not. No one does. Why do you want to become a Dutch citizen?"

"Pretty much the same reasons. I hate America."

"I'm not sure I would go that far. It's just embarrassing to me. But if I were your age, I would probably hate it."

He smiled at her a little at that moment. It wasn't much, but she thought she had made a good beginning, so she finished her hot water and got up.

"Well, I'm going to keep looking for decaf. Thanks for the conversation."

"Bye."

Often in their work, Charles and Louise had to begin relationships with people, and one of the principles they followed was to begin slowly. Usually, they believed, a first contact should be a smile, some recognition of similarity, a short conversation. Pushing a relationship too hard often alienated those involved. Also, at a certain point, they had to ask something of the person, something that tested the relationship. At this point, the subject might look back and review the history of time the two had spent together to see if there were signs of something wrong. A pushy beginning would fail this test.

Back in their flat they reviewed the first meeting and decided it was innocent enough to pass the test. As they listened in on conversations in the woonboot, they considered it meaningful that Arthur said nothing to the others about having met an American woman. It was a good sign. If he was going to keep a secret from them, or even just not mention it, it suggested the seed of a difference between him and the other cell members that could later turn more sharply into discord or separation.

"When should we make a second contact, do you think?" Louise asked.

"Not too quickly. Maybe a week."

"Yes. That was my thought too."

Chapter 17
The Dry Run

Meanwhile, something happened which neither the cell members nor the two Americans watching them expected. A signal came to Ibrahim. He was sitting on his bed, having just awakened, rubbing his eyes. His cell phone rang. He answered it quickly but with some apprehension.

"Hello?"

"Ibrahim?"

"Yes." His knees began to tremble.

"This is your uncle in Riyadh."

"Yes, Uncle."

It was their contact to Al Qaeda, one of a half-dozen men who were in contact through messengers with the Supreme Leader, hidden deep in a remote village in Pakistan. This half-dozen were the only ones authorized to send a signal to any of the many sleeper cells throughout the world. There were only two signals that they might send. One signal was to attack, and each cell had a particular target and a particular method of attack, learned and practiced during training, which they would use when the attack signal was received. The other signal was to perform a practice exercise, a dry run, and this was the signal Ibrahim received.

For each cell, the practice exercise was different, according to their target and the operation itself, but each cell knew that the practice run must include all the physical actions required in an actual attack except those that might expose the cell or its purpose, stopping just short of the final action. The details had been planned and memorized during their training. The group in Amsterdam had to go to the different places where the components of the bomb were located. They must do everything except actually pick up the components, then travel to the place where the components would be assembled, go through the motions of assembling and planting the device, then return to their woonboot in Amsterdam. Everything would be timed, and the few contacts they would make during the dry run with other cells and cell members would be used to evaluate their performance.

When Ibrahim heard the signal, he was much relieved, first that it was not Allah telling him he was going to be punished, then glad that it was only a dry run, which had little or no risk to it. Only, perhaps, and he trembled a little to think about it, Allah might object.

Charles and Louise, monitoring all cell phone traffic to and from the cell, also heard the call.

"Ibrahim," the uncle had said, "I hope you are all well and performing well in your studies. I understand that you will have an examination soon. I will be interested to hear the results."

"Yes, Uncle," Ibrahim had said. "I will let you know." And the conversation ended.

To Charles and Louise, it sounded like a signal. It was the first time the "uncle" had called and the conversation was too brief to be real. They had no idea what the signal meant, but they were sure it was a signal, and they immediately informed Henderson, who was in touch with his colleagues. But before they could put together a message to the Kuwaiti mole requesting clarification, he had found his way to an international phone booth and called his contact in Washington to tell him that they had been asked to do a dry run, which he explained in detail to his contact. This information was passed along to Henderson who emailed Charles and Louise. So, within a little more than a day they knew exactly what was going to happen.

Ibrahim and all the cell members knew from their training that the dry run was supposed to take place on exactly the third day after the signal was received, the same time interval that was allowed in the event of a signal to attack. Of course the Kuwaiti mole knew too that the dry run was to take place in three days, but he had not mentioned this to his handler in the excitement of the call, and now he was busy with the run itself.

The timing of the dry run became apparent when Akhmed called Takhmina and told her he would not be able to meet her as planned to study together in a downtown coffeehouse. As the two Americans listened in on conversations in the woonboot, the timing became even clearer. The cell members were to disperse at 6:00 in the morning for each of them to go through the motions of picking up his part of the bomb. Ibrahim had the important job of getting the explosive, which would be in an apartment in The Hague, near the target. He had to go there, knock on the door, and say his name. Those in the apartment knew that their job was simply to note his name and the time, which they would later phone in to "Uncle."

Akhmed had to go to an electrical store and buy a particular type of clock radio, which would be modified into a timing device, and some wiring and connectors, the last of which he had to hide inside a metal flute that he would carry in a flute case. His role was critical but easy enough to do so that he was not timed the way Ibrahim was. He did, however, have to show up at the assembly point at the right time.

Osama had the job of getting the detonator, and he had to go through the motions of picking it up in Rotterdam, and taking it in their car to the assembly point. He too would give his name, which would be phoned in, along with his pick-up time to the "uncle" in Riyadh.

Muhammad, Arthur, and Talgat had only to get themselves to the assembly point, where Muhammad's job was to make sure that the group was not disturbed during the assembly process, and he could use the Kuwaiti and the American as guards to help keep outsiders away. The ones who were to assemble the bomb—Ibrahim, Akhmed, and Osama—would meet in a public bathroom in the World Court building, and have seven minutes of undisturbed time there. Those keeping watch to make sure they had enough time were not to do anything that might alert anyone to the purpose of their activities. If it turned out that they could not provide the necessary seven minutes of privacy, the plan would then be altered or abandoned.

Chapter 18
The Tail

The terrorists reviewed their assignments in the woonboot the evening before the day of the run, and Charles and Louise, listening in, knew exactly who would be doing what. They planned their own activities accordingly. During the night, Charles carefully jimmied open the terrorists' car, popped the hood, and loosened one of the spark wires, so the engine would run roughly. He then closed the hood, placed an orange, without any drugs in it, on the passenger's seat and relocked the doors. Between the two items, he hoped Osama would be late in appearing at the apartment where the detonator was kept.

If there had been more time, they would have set up another meeting with Arthur/Anwar, but it would probably not have made much difference. As for Akhmed, there was nothing more they could do. His relationship with Takhmina, still in the earliest stage, would not be likely to influence his performance. For Ibrahim they planned on making another disturbing call. Charles had been studying the Holy Qur'an for a number of weeks and had identified several passages in which the Prophet's love of peace and dislike of violence and war were clearly set forth. Violence could be condoned only under certain circumstances, which the holy book described. He would quote them in his call to Ibrahim.

Five of the six men left the woonboot at exactly six o'clock in the morning, in the dark of a Dutch winter morning. The sun would not rise for another four hours, and at this time of year cloud cover was nearly always present and sunrise would be a slow change from black to opalescent gray. Osama chugged off in the car, nursing the engine along. They were by now used to the car not performing very well. Arthur/Anwar and the Kuwaiti mole went together by commuter train to the Central Amsterdam Station, where they boarded a train to The Hague. Muhammad took the same train but did not sit with them. They would all be early, but they had the job of looking over the entire building before the bomb components arrived to make sure that the building's security had not changed, that the bathroom they planned to use was not closed for repairs, and that the actual location for the bomb outside the court chambers, behind a small podium that was stored in a corner of the room, was still available to them. It was their job to make any small changes in the plot that might prove necessary and communicate them to the other cell members.

Ibrahim too took a train to The Hague, but he went a little later. He went first to the mosque, where he performed his morning prayers.

Charles and Louise had decided that Charles would follow Ibrahim, making sure to avoid detection by occasional changes in his appearance. Their hope was that by following him they would discover the address where he was to pick up the explosive. This address would certainly be one of the other cells of Al Qaeda in the Netherlands, and if it turned out to be one already known to the authorities, it would still be useful to know their role in this particular plot. If the address were not known, the information would be even more valuable.

So, when Ibrahim left the mosque and took a commuter train to the Central Station in Amsterdam, Charles was nearby, dressed in the blue coveralls of an aging Dutch worker, which he would later take off, stuff in a shopping bag he carried, and with the addition of a clip-on tie, take on the appearance of a retired civil servant or businessman.

Charles did not know, however, that someone else was also following Ibrahim. There was another man, dark, tall, evidently Middle Eastern, dressed well in Western style and clean-shaven, not far away. He was "Uncle," one of the six trusted colleagues of the Leader, and on this gray December morning, he was checking out the dry run of one of the Dutch cells. His job was to "run" all the cells in the Netherlands and Belgium, and it was a big job. The Leader had identified a dozen targets in these two countries and cells for each one had been trained. Some of the cells had plans to hijack aircraft, although the present level of airport security in these two countries made it unlikely that they could carry these plans out. The man following Ibrahim had been the one who sent the signal calling for the dry run. He did not, at first, realize that Charles was also following Ibrahim.

Louise had decided to follow Akhmed. Of course, she had to steer clear of Arthur/Anwar for fear that he might recognize her. So it was either Osama or Akhmed. Osama had the more important mission, and by following him she might be able to identify another cell, which might have yielded valuable information—but he was driving a car that they hoped would behave unpredictably, and that fact made following him very difficult. Without a second car to spell her she would probably have to abandon the tail if Osama's car broke down. So, she decided to trail Akhmed. She hoped to learn more about how the operation was supposed to work and transmit her discoveries to the home office.

Akhmed had to buy some equipment and had to wait for the stores to open. He could have bought these innocuous items earlier and kept them in the woonboot, but the instructions to the cell were clear: to get all of the bomb components on the same day that the plot, or in this case the dry run, was carried out. They didn't question the authority, and they did understand the reasoning behind it. So Akhmed waited for an hour before leaving the woonboot, and then got himself a nice breakfast in the restaurant of the train station before leaving for The Hague at 8:00. As the train approached The Hague, Akhmed was thinking about Takhmina. He was often thinking about

Takhmina these days. He had promised her that he would call her around the time of the meeting that he had had to cancel, so he placed the call on his cell phone from the train. Takhmina answered, and they began one of those rambling conversations that lovers, or potential lovers, have, which have little in the way of content but serve only to maintain contact with the other person. He was so engrossed in the conversation that he did not get off at The Hague station, and he didn't realize his mistake until the train was pulling out of the station. The next station was 15 minutes away, where he would have to get off, cross to the other side, wait for a return train, and retrace his path for an additional 15 minutes. All of this meant that he would be about 45 minutes behind schedule, and he was visibly agitated, so much so that a woman sitting next to him changed her seat. He was hoping he could make up some of the lost time in The Hague when he went to buy the alarm clock and the wiring. Of course, he thought, it wasn't necessary to actually buy anything. Osama and Ibrahim were not going to bring any actual components. He could skip the trip to the electrical store and arrive on time, lying to them about his trip and about missing the station. There was a hidden consequence to his deception, however—he felt a little more alienated from the cell than he had before. It was a small change, but important.

Chapter 19
The Birds

Muhammad, Arthur, and Talgat, the security detail, arrived at the World Court building at opening time, as planned, and proceeded to check it out. Each one had his particular assignment, and carried them out efficiently, riding the elevator to each of the floors, walking the public corridors, and varying their route so that they did not appear suspicious, until finally they all met at a café in the building and pronounced everything OK. Then they ordered coffee and breakfast, which they ate while waiting the additional half hour. For them, everything was on schedule.

For Osama, things did not go so well. The trip to Rotterdam took longer than planned. The car would not go more than 40 mph, and before long he realized he would be late for his pretend pickup of the detonator. As he muttered to himself about the delay, his hand fell to the seat next to him and landed on the orange. He picked it up and looked at it in surprise. He was sure he had not put it there. As soon as his fingers wrapped themselves around the dimpled skin, his hallucinations about birds flying in his face returned. They were never as severe as on that first morning—there were fewer birds—but the birds he saw seemed very real and he could not help swatting at them as he drove.

As he was doing this, a German-licensed Mercedes came up behind him at about 100 mph, and had to slam on its brakes to keep from hitting him. It slowed to 60 before pulling around him, then, shouting German curses that Osama couldn't hear, cut him off by pulling very close in front of him as a way of expressing anger. Osama slammed on his brakes and the car swerved to the side. He was holding the wheel with one hand and swatting birds with the other. Momentarily, he lost control and drifted off to the shoulder, and then to the snowy area beyond the shoulder. The car skidded a little, climbed the berm left by the snowplow and came to rest straddling it. The engine stalled.

Osama got the engine started again, although it was still rough, but the car would not move. The wheels spun in the snow; the undercarriage resting partly on the berm reduced the traction between the wheels and the icy ground. Osama banged his hands on the wheel in frustration, then giggled. He got out and tried to clear the snow away, so that the wheels could get a grip, but nothing seemed to work. He gave up and got back in the car.

In 20 minutes, an official Dutch traffic car, but not the police, spotted him and pulled over. They offered to call a tow truck, and he accepted. He really needed only a little push, but the official said she couldn't do that without damaging their car. Fifteen minutes later the tow truck arrived, and the driver got out and approached Osama. There wasn't much to say; it was obvious what had happened, but it would have been very impolite not to give greetings. The driver heard the engine of the little Opel and asked Osama to open the hood. Then he asked him to turn the engine off, and while it was off he replaced the wire that Charles had loosened. When Osama started the car back up, it sounded fine. The tow truck inched up behind him with its massive wooden bumper and nudged him off the berm. They waved goodbye and Osama was back on the road, now doing 65; the car was running better than ever.

He'd lost half an hour, and he'd already been 10 minutes behind schedule, so he continued to drive as fast as he dared toward the meeting in Rotterdam. He was late and gave his name, giggling. The people in the apartment simply said OK and waved him off. But they noted the time, and they made some comments in their report that he was out of breath, and seemed immature.

Chapter 20
The Failure

Ibrahim finished praying and left the mosque. He went to the Central Station and caught the next train to The Hague. He had plenty of time. As he rode along, looking a little nervously at the flat Dutch countryside, his cell phone rang.

"Hello?"

"Ah Ibrahim," said that deep voice.

Ibrahim's hand holding the cell phone next to his ear began to tremble.

"Yes?"

"Ibrahim. Read Holy Qur'an 2, 208. Read also Surat al-Ma'ida, 48. And heed the words carefully."

The line went dead. He had the Holy Qur'an with him, and he found the passages easily. They described the Prophet's dislike of violence and praised men of peace. He looked deeply troubled as he read the passages over three times, and put the holy book away. He began to breathe rapidly.

He arrived a little early at the place where he was to pick up the explosive and knocked on the door. A heavy-set, darkly Arabic man opened the door and asked him brusquely what he wanted. Ibrahim identified himself, but stumbled in his speech and spoke so softly that the man asked him to repeat his name. He did so, then turned from the door and walked slowly away. The man watched through his window as Ibrahim walked away on the street, shaking his head. Ibrahim felt deeply sad, as if his heart was torn. He was troubled almost to the point of breakdown. The contact man saw the slow, dejected walk and made several notes in a book.

Charles had followed a full block behind Ibrahim. There were not many people in the street, and he could not follow more closely without avoiding detection. When Ibrahim entered the building, Charles couldn't see which apartment he went to. "Too bad," he thought. Henderson would have liked the information, but even without it, there was value in knowing the street address of another Al Qaeda operative. Not far away from Charles, Uncle realized that Charles was following Ibrahim and decided to stop following Ibrahim and to start following Charles. He could get timing and other information later from those in the apartment. He wondered "Who is this old person, and why is he following one of our cell members?" The Saudi was quite baffled. He was sure that Charles could not be a CIA man; they were always young, fit, and extremely confident. He re-examined his observations. Could he have been mistaken that the old man was following their cell member? No, there was no question. The old man was careful to follow at a certain distance, slowing down and speeding up the pace whenever Ibrahim did so. And it was clear that he was doing his best to avoid detection, moving into doorways when there was the possibility of the cell member seeing him, and once he changed from one hat to another, an action that could not be explained in any other way. Had the U.S. government become so weak that they used old men as spies? He had no answers to these questions, but he wanted to get to the bottom of the mystery. If the cell had been identified, it would have to be disbanded.

Ibrahim, after leaving the apartment, followed the plan. He didn't like what he was doing, but he was afraid of Al Qaeda almost as much as he was afraid of Allah. So he arrived at the World Court building in The Hague on time. In the event of a real attack, he would have had the explosives strapped around his middle. They did not have radar or dogs at the Court, and even if he had been carrying the actual explosive, he would pass the metal detectors. The detonator device was made of plastic and very small, so Osama would also get through. Only the timing device would have metal in it, and they had planned to have the alarm clock wrapped as a gift. Even if opened, it was still only an alarm clock and would not excite more than passing suspicion. The wires, however, were highly suspicious, but they were to be placed inside a silver flute that Akhmed would carry, and although the flute would be seen, the wires would be hidden inside it. But of course this was only a dry run, and none of them was carrying anything.

When Ibrahim arrived, he went directly to the bathroom, where he found Talgat, Anwar, and Muhammad in place but no sign of Osama or Akhmed. They all waited, doing nothing for ten minutes. Then Akhmed arrived, out of breath from running; he'd come straight from the train station and not stopped long enough to buy the alarm clock and the wires, nor to place the wires inside the flute, but his cohorts didn't know that.

"Where is Osama?" Ibrahim asked.

There was no answer, and Ibrahim's shoulders shrugged in grateful resignation. "Perhaps it is not meant to be."

They waited for another ten minutes, and then Ibrahim said the word that scrubbed the practice run. All of them were dejected. They had failed. They left the building separately, as planned, and traveled separately back to Amsterdam. Osama arrived at the Court building 35 minutes late and missed all of them. It was obvious that the mission had been scrubbed and he went back to Amsterdam convinced that his tardiness was the main reason. But he didn't feel guilty about it. He had a good explanation for everything that had happened to him. He wondered, however, if the rest of his cohorts would believe him. Their instructions for the dry run, as well as for the real thing, said not to use their cell phones, so he couldn't have called anyone to explain. Later they would have a chance to talk, and Osama could tell his story of the slow car and getting stuck in the snow.

Chapter 21
The Uncle

Uncle had made the decision to follow Charles, so when Charles decided to stop following Ibrahim and head for home, the tall Arab was not far behind him as he walked up to the train station and waited on the platform. When he boarded the train, Charles was still unaware of Uncle, sitting in the same car with him. He saw, however, that Louise was in the car, sitting all the way at the other end, and he wondered how she'd gotten there and why she didn't just come up to the front of the car and sit with him. But Charles was a well-seasoned agent and realized that something was going on. Certainly, Louise had some reason for her behavior. So he sat in his seat and waited.

Louise had come to be on the train with Uncle and Charles as a result of losing Akhmed when he failed to get off the train at The Hague. She'd been sitting in the car behind his. By getting up and walking to the front of the car she could see where he was sitting, and she did this as the train pulled into the station, but when she looked he wasn't in his seat, and she assumed that he was standing by the doors waiting to get out. Actually, he'd changed his seat earlier to get more privacy for his conversation with Takhmina.

Consequently, when she got off the train and looked around, she couldn't see Akhmed anywhere. But she saw Charles, and as she looked ahead of him she saw Ibrahim whom he was following. It was then that she realized that a tall, dark-skinned man seemed to be following Charles. Uncle had already noticed Ibrahim's odd behavior, and to see also that he was being followed by a westerner completely disgusted the Al Qaeda operative. The cell seemed to be falling apart, a conclusion he reached without knowing anything about the mishaps of Akhmed and Osama. He decided to follow Charles as well as Ibrahim. So, as Ibrahim approached the World Court, a string of three people followed him, although Louise, being the last, was the only one who knew it.

When Charles decided that there was no point in following Ibrahim any farther and turned around, Uncle took refuge in a shop. Louise thought it best at that moment not to reveal her presence to Charles. Doing so would have increased the risk of Uncle spotting her as well. She slipped into a café, where she could keep her eye on Uncle as Charles went by, headed for the train station. Uncle stepped out of the shop a few moments afterwards, and then, after an interval, Louise resumed following Uncle. All three of them had reversed course. It reminded her of a Keystone Kops movie, and it would have been funny if it were not for the very serious business they were engaged in.

When they got to the train station, Louise kept well out of sight until the train came, then got on several cars behind Charles and Uncle who had gotten onto the same car. Then she worked her way through the train until she could see through the door window of the car where each of them was sitting. She counted the seat rows between them then went back to her seat and called Charles on her cell phone. Charles jumped a little when the cell phone rang, then said hello.

"It's me," said Louise. "There's a guy on the train following you. He's tall, Arabic-looking, seated eight rows behind you on the right side of the train. I'm in the car behind yours."

"OK." Charles took this all in quickly, processed the information, and began to think of strategies. Louise had hung up. But she got up and walked to the connecting platform to look into the other car.

Charles had two thoughts. First, in his training he was taught that offense is better than defense, so he was inclined to take the initiative. His second thought was that he had recently been quite successful at playing God. He got up and walked back in the car, heading straight for Uncle, who saw him coming and suddenly became interested in his fingernails. When he looked up, he was surprised to find Charles standing next to him, staring at him silently. As soon as they had made eye contact, Charles began speaking to him in Arabic, using the flowery, ancient forms of Holy Qur'an, and spouting off some of the same verses he had directed Ibrahim to read.

"A man of peace is respected above all others. Violence does harm too those who use it; it is an abomination to the Lord. Be not afraid to seek redress through negotiation. The tribal leader who..."

"Who are you, and why do you speak to me in this manner?"

Charles blinked hard, and allowed his knees to buckle, catching himself on the seatback, then spoke in English.

"Excuse me. Was I speaking to you? What was I saying? I, I, I'm sorry if I disturbed you," and he started to turn away. But Uncle grabbed his arm, and turned him back so that they were once again face to face.

"Who are you?" Uncle repeated.

"James Benson, International Herald Tribune," Charles said, extending his hand.

But Uncle ignored the hand.

"Why do you speak to me in this old Arabic?"

"I'm sorry, but I don't speak Arabic. Perhaps you're confusing me with someone else." Charles looked around him.

"You were speaking to me in Arabic."

"No. I don't speak Arabic. I'm of—" At this moment, Charles rolled his eyes back in his head, made his whole body rigid, and rattled off the same Koranic verses he had before, ending them with "Thus, thou seeest. I speak to thee through this infidel."

Uncle's eyes widened and his hand shook.

"I, I...." Uncle was for the moment unable to speak.

Then Charles let his knees buckle again and allowed himself to fall to the floor. People nearby gasped. Louise came into the car and up to Charles, who was "reviving." She wasn't sure what had happened, but as soon as Charles began to revive, she immediately knew he was playing a part, and joined him in it.

"It's OK. I'm a nurse," she said getting to Charles' side and helping him to his feet in the swaying train.

"How are you?" she said.

"Did I fall?"

"I'm not sure what happened. Maybe you had some kind of seizure." She looked at the Arab. "Did you do something to this man?"

"No. No, I do not know him."

"He's lying," said one of the passengers. "The older man was speaking to him in another language."

"So you do know him," Louise said accusingly to Uncle.

"No. I do not know him. Yes, he was speaking to me in Arabic, but I do not know him."

Charles recognized an odor coming from the Arab, and he suddenly stiffened his body, as he had before. "Fornicator!" he shouted in Arabic, "Fornicator with young boys. Thou must forbear this practice. It is forbidden to Muslims."

Uncle looked shocked. "How did you know..." His voice trailed off as he realized he was revealing something about himself that he didn't want known.

Charles, still standing stiffly, continued in very loud Arabic. "Thou hast drunk alcohol and fornicated with boys. This will be punished." With this, he rolled his eyes back in his head and let his legs buckle, but Louise was holding him, and he steadied himself on the seatback again.

"I, I'm sorry. I must be disturbing you," Charles said in a quiet English voice. "Was I speaking to you?"

"Who are you?" Uncle asked. His voice shook.

"James Benson, International Herald Tribune." His hand extended.

"Why do you speak to me this way?"

"I'm sorry, I, I don't know what was happening. Did I faint?"

Louise said to him "I think we should get you to a seat." She guided Charles, turning him away and walking him to a nearby empty seat, looking back reproachfully at Uncle, who sat now, staring straight ahead, trying not to notice the people staring at him. He hoped that none of them spoke Arabic.

The woman next to him said, "What did he say to you?"

He looked at her for a long time, but he did not answer.

Louise got up and walked back to where Uncle was seated. "May I have your name and address? I will need it for my report to the doctor."

"I...No, you may not." He tried to look indignant, but he was still quite flustered from the loud accusations in Arabic.

"But then it will become a matter for the police."

"No. I do not have to give you my name."

Other passengers were now staring at him with some hostility. Louise, meanwhile, was taking out her camera, and was just getting it ready when Uncle realized what she was going to do and put his hands over his face. Passengers began to nod as if they understood. One of them said "He's probably one of those terrorists." She said this in Dutch, and some of the passengers looked alarmed. One of them repeated the word "terrorist." The woman next to Uncle looked more alarmed than any. "I want to get out," she said. "Let me out." She pulled and jerked on his sleeve. He got up, and as he did so his hands came away from his face, and Louise took a picture. Immediately, he lunged for her camera, but she had anticipated the movement, and had dropped it in her purse and turned away from him, clutching her purse with both hands.

"Give me that!" he shouted.

"Help!" Louise shouted, running toward the front of the car. Uncle was after her, determined to get her purse. As he passed the seat where Charles was sitting, Charles extended his foot, and Uncle sprawled on the floor of the aisle. A male passenger jumped on his back. A policeman appeared. The man got off Uncle and gestured to the policeman to handcuff him, which the policeman was about to do.

"He was trying to take her purse," a passenger said to the policeman gesturing toward Louise. Other passengers nodded. The policeman was convinced. He put cuffs on Uncle and stood him up. At the next stop, the policeman, Uncle and Louise all got off. Charles went too, although the policeman had not yet seen Charles' connection to the incident.

The policeman took out a little book. He carried on his shoulder a little walkie-talkie, and he spoke into it rapidly in Dutch, informing someone in a more central location of what was going on. "Now," he said in English to the foreigners, looking at Uncle, "what's your name?"

Uncle sighed and with his cuffed hands fished his wallet out of his hip pocket. He turned his back toward the policeman to give him the passport, which Charles noted had Arabic lettering on it, although he was unable to make out the country. Uncle was trying hard not to say his name out loud. Once Louise had asked for it he began to think that she might be an agent of some kind. He was very confused, but he knew enough not to say his name out loud if he could help it.

The policeman scrutinized the passport, looking for the English spelling. "Ah, here. Hassan ibn Azamat. Is that correct?"

Uncle nodded sullenly. The policeman made a note. "Where do you stay in Holland?"

"At the American Hotel in Amsterdam."

"May I see your room key?"

"I left it."

"Your room assignment then."

He produced a paper and handed it to the policeman.

"143," the policeman said. Hassan ibn Azamat rolled his eyes and nearly stamped his foot in frustration. Then the policeman turned to Louise.

"And you are whom?" he said in his best English.

"Karen Wethersfield. I'm a photographer for the International Herald Tribune," she said, showing him her passport and press card. The policeman made more notes. Hassan looked even more alarmed. He remembered that Louise had said she was a nurse, but now she was saying she was a journalist. He didn't like the change. He was sure that she was a spy, but she too looked too old to be a CIA person. Then the policeman turned to Charles, who gave his reporter's identity and presented his papers on request.

"Who can tell me what happened?"

Louise raised her hand, and Hassan raised one of his cuffed hands as best he could. Charles half-raised his, hesitating.

"You begin." He gestured to Hassan.

"This man," he said, pointing to Charles, "came up to me and began shouting in Arabic, saying terrible things to me."

"I don't speak Arabic," Charles said, "but I think that I may have been speaking to this man. I'm really not sure. I believe I fainted, or, or, perhaps he hit me. I don't know. I introduced myself to him."

The policeman gave a hard look at Hassan. "Show me your hands."

Hassan turned, and the policeman inspected his knuckles, then made some notes in his little book.

"It does not look as though he hit you."

"Then perhaps I fainted. I don't really remember."

The policeman turned to Louise. "What did you see?"

"I heard shouting behind me and turned. My partner," she pointed at Charles, "was lying on the floor. He began to revive as

I went up to him. I pretended to be a nurse so that I could get close to him."

"Why were you not sitting together?"

"We see more that way. We are reporters."

"I see. Did you hear what was shouted?"

"I heard, but it was not a language I understand."

"It was Arabic. He spoke to me in classical Arabic," said Hassan.

"In classical Arabic? What is that?"

"Old Arabic, like that in Holy Qur'an."

"And you do not speak this language?" he said, turning to Charles.

"Certainly not. I am an American. I know only a little French from high school. I do not speak even modern Arabic."

Hassan's eyes seemed to widen at this statement. He was beginning to be convinced that Charles was telling the truth about his language skills, and that meant that Allah may have been speaking through him. It frightened him.

"Do you want to press charges against this man?" the policeman asked.

"No." Charles answered quickly.

The policeman looked at Louise. "How about you, Miss Wethersfield? Do you want to press charges?"

"Well, he did try to take my purse. But he didn't get it. So, no, I guess not."

The policeman turned Hassan around and uncuffed him. "Do not change your address without letting us know. You are free to go."

Hassan walked quickly away. He was now upset on two counts. He was now known to the police, and to this old American couple, and they knew where he was staying. He knew that he would be identified quickly, and they would know him to be a member of Al Qaeda. He had to leave the country as quickly as possible.

The policeman indicated that Charles and Louise should stay with him until this apparently dangerous man was out of sight. Then he turned to them, but before he could say anything, Charles pulled out his other set of identification papers and showed them. The policeman's eyes widened.

"May I speak to your Chief?" asked Charles. "It is quite urgent."

The policeman saw the official U.S. Embassy stamp on Charles papers, and pressed a button on the intercom attached to his shoulder, turning so that Charles could speak into it. Charles spoke to the Chief, using a code word that made the Chief listen very carefully. The Chief then asked to speak with the officer, who with a gesture indicated that Charles and Louise were not needed for any further questioning.

Charles immediately placed a call to the U.S. Embassy and, using his own code word, was switched to an attaché who was responsible for anti-terrorism efforts in the Netherlands. Charles explained the situation to him and gave him Hassan's name, and said where he was staying in Amsterdam.

Hassan considered going straight to the airport, or renting a car and driving out of the Netherlands without going back to his hotel, but he had become used to a softer way of life, and he wanted to get his things. Also, there were in his hotel room some very incriminating pictures that showed him doing unspeakable things with two young boys he had hired for the night. He did not want anyone to see them. It had been a serious mistake. He entered the hotel and rushed to his room, eager to destroy the evidence of his indiscretion and to get out of the country.

When he got to his room, however, he opened the door and found his room full of strange men. He tried to back out the door and run, but there was an agent in the hallway who had been hiding in a recess near the elevator. He was arrested by representatives of the American government in cooperation with the Dutch police and taken to the American Embassy, where there was a small holding cell. He was not permitted to make any calls. He was, in fact, a very big fish to catch, one of the few men who still had access to the new Leader. The news of his capture was not announced because the Americans believed that they might get some more information about his boss if they kept it quiet.

When Charles and Louise got back to their apartment, they found email messages from Henderson, congratulating them on what was one of the most important events in the "war on terror," although it would not be made known to the public for quite some time.

"We were really very lucky," Louise said.

"Maybe so, but you spotted Hassan in the first place," Charles said.

"And you showed a lot of chutzpah in approaching him," she said.

"All right, we both deserve some credit for it," Charles said.

They took out their instruments and played some old Woody Guthrie tunes: "Curly Headed Baby" and "Oklahoma Hills." The harmonica riffs accentuated the rhythm of horses' hooves that they always heard in these songs. The easy music brought them down, cooled them off, and slid them smoothly into bed. Louise was always excited by danger, and Charles made the most of it. They made love slowly and tenderly, smiling at each other, and whispering their names to each other. Then they slept deeply and long, not far from the woonboot.

Chapter 22
The Money

The next day, they received a call from Henderson.

"The people in counter-intelligence want to find out when and how other Al Qaeda leaders become aware of Hassan's absence, so they are keeping the news of his capture quiet. This will give them an opportunity to assess Al Qaeda's reaction to it."

"All right. We understand that," Charles replied.

"Is there a timeline?" Louise asked.

"Not really," Henderson replied. He went on to explain. "There may be no reaction at all. Al Qaeda has changed its structure several times since 9/11. It is not as rigidly structured as it was, so it may be that the other "uncles" will never know that one of their members has been taken."

"But then how will 'our' cell keep going?" Charles asked.

"There is one other person, higher up in the Al Qaeda hierarchy, who will know that Hassan has disappeared, and that another 'uncle' will have to take over his part of the operation." Henderson said.

"And that person will report to his superior," Louise offered.

"Exactly," Henderson said.

"So, eventually, the men in the woonboot will hear from their new uncle," Louise said.

"Yes," said Henderson, "but this will take time, and we aren't sure how much."

"So, for some uncertain period, there will be no directions for the cell," Charles said.

"Right," Henderson said.

"We have a window of opportunity," Louise said, "when the cell will be drifting along, waiting for directions."

"It will provide a better chance for us to work on chipping away at their unity and morale," Charles offered.

"And perhaps some advancement toward your new mission—to break the cell up altogether," Henderson said. "We have already made a beginning on that," Charles said, ending the conference call on an optimistic note.

And he was right. Ibrahim, who was the eldest and the natural leader of the group, was very close to packing it in. After the dry run's failure, he went through the motions of leadership, but took no specific action beyond deciding on the minor issues that came up in their university courses, food purchases, and the other mechanics of life in Amsterdam. He stayed with the group only because he was afraid of Al Qaeda, afraid that if he simply abandoned the woonboot, they or someone else would track him down and kill him.

Charles and Louise, meeting in their now-favorite café, were brainstorming.

"We've already opened a crack in their cohesiveness," Louise said. "Now we have to wedge something into the crack."

"We might be able to make the whole thing fall apart," Charles said optimistically. "At the first sign of disintegration, I think Ibrahim would leave the group and try to find his own way. I'm sure he wouldn't mind being a martyr, but I'll bet that he doesn't believe now that setting off a bomb in the World Court would result in his martyrdom. In fact, he thinks now that it would be against God's will."

"That's great. I hope you're right," said Louise.

"What about Akhmed and Takhmina?" Charles asked.

"They've progressed only a short way into their relationship," Louise said. "But he is fixated on her. I'll bet he thinks about her all the time, and wants to be with her as much as possible."

"Do you think he sees her as a path to freedom from the straitjacket of his former life?"

"Maybe. We know that he grew up poor in Saudi Arabia with his two brothers. And being poor in Saudi Arabia, in the midst of enormous wealth, would make anyone angry and resentful."

"Everything he and Osama and Muhammad were taught in the madras in Riyadh fueled their resentment against America."

"And religion threw more fuel on that fire."

"Exactly."

"But now," Charles suggested, "he's discovering that rage against poverty and the ice-cold helplessness that accompanies it can be melted in the warm breeze of possibility."

"I like that metaphor," said Louise.

"Thanks," Charles said. "It seemed descriptive. But what about Osama? He came from the same background."

"Osama's situation is different," Louise said. "He has the same rage against the U.S., but when he began to see birds flying in his face, his brothers and his cousin all turned against him."

"He seemed to think it was funny at first."

"Well, it was funny—a terrorist cell being attacked by imaginary birds—but in time, I think he began to feel isolated, cut off from the cell, which is the only support he's ever known."

"I see," Charles said. "And as their suspicion of his sanity continues, his loneliness should grow."

"I don't think they believe he is crazy any more. Still, they don't trust him as much as they used to, and that will also make him feel different and cut off."

"Even though his reactions to the hallucinations have stopped?"

"They went on long enough for the other members of the cell to lose confidence in his stability and maturity. It's the loss of their confidence that he feels and resents, I think."

"He probably couldn't explain it to them."

"No, he couldn't. He had no idea where his odd behavior had come from in the first place."

"He probably even wondered himself if he was not a little crazy."

"Could be."

"And Muhammad?" Charles asked.

Louise wrinkled her brow, not sure what the answer to Charles' question was.

"What does it say in the folder?"

Louise retrieved the folder and read about Muhammad for a few minutes, then looked up and summarized what she had read.

"He's the youngest, and before his parents died, they gave him a lot of special attention. So, the authors of the dossier surmise that he felt less deprived by poverty than his brothers and it was harder for him to feel angry. Instead, they think he was simply lost and lonely, an orphan by the time he was a teenager. He transferred the dependence he felt toward his parents onto his two older brothers and his cousin Ibrahim, who had become like a father to all three brothers. Muhammad followed his brothers into Al Qaeda with the same 'me too' feeling he'd had when he followed them into soccer games. And at the madras, he went through the motions of hating American, but without much conviction."

"So he'll probably just go along with whatever his brothers do."

"That would be my guess."

"OK. That leaves Arthur/Anwar."

"He's a much harder case. His anti-Americanism was bred in the bone. No need to add fuel to the fire of his anger. But I think it's worth a try to see if he responds to a surrogate parental relationship. Even if all we do is respond to his need to be accepted by an older person, one who listens and accepts him as he is, it might prevent him from doing something awful. There is still the possibility that if we succeed in breaking up the cell, Arthur will go off and perform some terrorist act independently."

So, Louise made sure that she "ran into" him again at the same café and, in her best clinical manner, simply listened without judgment to everything he said. She made it look as though their schedules coincided so that they often ate lunch together, and at each lunch, she listened. Occasionally, she offered an opinion of her own, carefully chosen and worded so as to be compatible with his ideas but a little more reserved, conservative, thoughtful, and wise. In other words, when she presented herself, it was as a parent. She did this quite naturally. As a therapist, she'd been accustomed to finding within herself qualities and characteristics, which became whole roles, totally genuine and true to herself, yet very much what her patients needed to relate to. Seeing Arthur became a part of her daily routine.

It was a major triumph, she felt, when he told her that his original name had been Arthur, and when she asked if it would be all right for her to call him that instead of Anwar, he had agreed, a shy smile spreading across his face. She knew then that she had penetrated his defenses. She kept a daily record of her encounters with him, just as if he were one of her patients in the days when she was a practicing therapist.

Charles took on some of the tasks Louise had done before the Arthur Campaign, as they came to call it. He was now in charge of monitoring the group's cell phone use, and the flow of their money into and out of the bank account. The latter endeavor was of particular interest to them both, because of the arrest of Hassan. He had been the one who transferred monthly sums from an account in Saudi Arabia to the cell's bank account in Amsterdam. Now that he was "unavailable" to do this, Charles and Louise had to make a decision. They could have, through computer shenanigans that Louise was a master of, made the transfers themselves, ensuring the continued financial well-being of the cell while they continued their efforts to undermine its morale and cohesiveness. Or, they could do nothing, so that the cell's money ran out, and they would try to get more. After consultation with Henderson, they decided on the latter course. It would minimize the chance that Al Qaeda would discover Louise's hacking—no one was sure how sophisticated their computer knowledge was. Also, it might help reveal some new information about the functioning, and perhaps even the individuals, involved in the higher levels of the organization.

So they waited, and when the time came for bills to be paid, the money ran out. The bank, having found itself in error previously, was very careful to document the shortfall before they called Ibrahim. He was, of course, sure that once again the stupid Dutch bank would discover that it had been wrong, and he pursued this line of thinking in his discussions with the bank officials for quite some time. But they were prepared for it and documented their case so well that he was, in the end, forced to concede and place another call to Uncle. But when he did, no one answered. The call was recorded on a computer in the U.S. Embassy that had been programmed to monitor all of the calls that came in to Hassan's phone, even though these calls were not answered. Ibrahim tried to call him several times each day over the next couple of days, and then the group in the woonboot became nervous. Without money, they would have to leave the country and return to Saudi Arabia, where they were not sure what kind of welcome they would receive.

Chapter 23
The Emergency

Their nervousness grew and Ibrahim called a meeting. They met in the living room of the woonboot, and Charles and Louise were listening in.

"It's another mistake," Ibrahim assured the group. "Eventually, the bank will see its mistake."

"But why hasn't Uncle answered?" asked Anwar. "That cannot be a mistake of the bank."

"No, of course not. It is something else. Perhaps he is away on a trip." This was Akhmed.

"Yes," Osama offered. "We are not the only group he attends to."

They all looked at Osama. What he said was true, but they doubted Osama, and didn't want to believe him.

"Does he also handle other groups like ours?" Muhammad wanted to know, directing his question at Ibrahim.

"I do not know the innermost workings of the organization. I was trained in the same way you were, but it is my belief that Uncle runs other groups besides ours."

"When we trained, there were three other groups there," said Muhammad. "Perhaps they are all the groups that Uncle deals with."

"That's possible," said Talgat, the mole, knowing that it was probably false, but interested in creating a false understanding wherever he could do so in apparent innocence.

"Was Uncle present at our training, do you think?" asked Akhmed.

"Several men came and observed us. You remember. And they looked like important people. Perhaps one of them was Uncle," said Ibrahim.

"Perhaps," said Osama. "But what does this mean?"

Akhmed and Muhammad looked at him as though he was to be pitied. He could not even follow the conversation.

"It means," said Akhmed with exaggerated patience, slowing his speech down, "that Uncle has other groups to think about and is away doing something with one of them."

"But the number you call—Uncle's number—is a cell phone number," said Anwar, throwing up his hands in disgust at the stupidity of the rest of them. "He doesn't have to be anywhere to answer the phone. It is with him."

All four of the al-Ryadis looked angrily at Anwar. Ibrahim spoke for them. "It is not appropriate for you to talk to us in this tone of voice, Anwar. It is not only Americans who understand technology." The al-Ryadi heads nodded together.

"I meant only that it is not simply that he is away. There is a more important reason why he does not answer his phone." Anwar was aware—indeed, he was constantly reminded—that he was an outsider, and he was trying at this moment to mend fences.

"Do you believe then that we should use the emergency number?" Akhmed asked.

"Eventually, we will have to," answered Anwar. "The question is, how long do we wait?" He looked for approval to Ibrahim, hoping he had not voiced an opinion that was above his station in the group.

There was a number, a number that only Ibrahim knew. He had memorized it during training. It was a number they were to use only in the event of an emergency. Each of them had been carefully taught what an "emergency" was and one of the things on the list was a loss of contact with their "uncle." So they knew Anwar's statement was accurate, but they hesitated. None of them wanted to acknowledge that they were in an emergency. They knew that the dry run had not gone well, but it was their first. They could improve. They knew too that some other things were not going well—Osama might be a little crazy, and Ibrahim had grown more and more religious—but was that bad or good? Akhmed's behavior had changed too, but it did not yet seem like a threat to the group. And the other bad things that had been happening to them lately seemed simply like bad luck. But in any case, they would eventually need money.

Ibrahim himself, who alone had the authority to decide that they were in an emergency, was reluctant for another reason: he simply was afraid to use the cell phone to call another number, a number that must be connected to an even higher level of authority than "Uncle." He was afraid of who might answer such a call.

So they waited for nearly a week, telling the bank that they were having some difficulty contacting their relatives at home. The bank was quite used to situations like this with foreigners and did not hesitate to grant them more time.

During this week, Akhmed met secretly with Takhmina several times. He had decided not to tell even his brothers about her because he was afraid—and justifiably so—that they would not share his enthusiasm for her, and would see it as something that diminished his loyalty to the cell. Probably they would not have approved of her more modern ways. Women were best not educated at all, much less to the advanced level that Takhmina sought. Akhmed's unexplained absences were, however, noticed by the others.

Arthur/Anwar met also with Louise, or Karen, as he called her. He did not consciously try to keep his meetings with the older American woman a secret, but he also did not go out of his way to tell the others about her. The distinction between not telling them and keeping a secret from them was a fiction he created in his own mind. His friendship with her had begun in such a simple way, luck really, and then their schedules happened to coincide, so it was more as though they kept running into each other. Nevertheless, he came to feel that his lunchtime meetings with the older American woman were an island of calm, comfortable relaxation surrounded by a sea of anger, turbulence, and stern dedication. It was his time, and he didn't want to share it. He did not see it as subversive, but he should have. It was undermining his hardness as surely as the spring sun melts the frozen ground and allows new growth. But he didn't. He just enjoyed it.

Chapter 24
The Funding

Akhmed and Takhmina met in a coffee shop overlooking the Prinsengracht. It was a more upscale place than either of them would have gone to on their own, but each was interested in impressing the other. They avoided talking about the future; it might have been embarrassing. Neither felt certain about their relationship, although for different reasons. So they talked about themselves as they were now. She was very forthright, but Akhmed was not. He couldn't, of course, tell her about the woonboot, at least not about the group's purpose, and she soon sensed his reluctance.

"I would like to meet your brothers and your cousin," she said.

"I would like that too," Akhmed said, "but at the moment I do not think they would approve of you."

"Why not?" She asked indignantly, for she felt that, if anything, she might be a little too good for this poor Saudi boy.

"Because you are not Saudi," Akhmed said, putting a nationalistic spin on her more modern, even western ways. He was, after all, still trying to woo her, and he put everything to her in the best possible light. "My brothers and my cousin are very old-fashioned." This was true, if you looked at it from her perspective, nor did it hurt to take some of the blame. "In time, I am sure they will come around to my point of view."

This last comment implied that Akhmed had already discussed Takhmina with his brothers and Ibrahim. He regretted the falsehood but saw no way to avoid it. He could not even imagine his brothers or Ibrahim seeing his relationship with Takhmina "from his point of view." In fact, as his feelings toward her deepened, he imagined them together in a beautiful, distant land—Denmark, perhaps, although he had never been there—but only the two of them. His brothers and Ibrahim were not a part of his fantasy. At the same time, he had not reached a point where he could consider leaving the cell. The practicalities, the strategy, for taking such a step were complex and dangerous, he believed. He didn't want to think about it.

Osama too had shifted slightly in his relationship to the group, but not as much as Akhmed and Anwar. He was beginning to feel isolated. They no longer consulted him on anything important, and when he offered an opinion to the group, they usually discounted it. He had at first understood this; he had behaved very peculiarly, and he was aware now of how peculiar it had been. But he had been acting normally now for weeks. Sure, occasionally he would see one or two birds, but he did his best not to react to them flying in his face, and sometimes he succeeded in not raising his hand to bat them away. But they no longer disrupted his behavior anymore, or so he thought. His performance in the dry run was awful, but it was the car's fault, and he couldn't have prevented it. Nevertheless, they continued to be suspicious of him and worried about his stability. Gradually, the isolation made him angry, particularly at Arthur/Anwar who seemed to blame him for his halucinations. When he had the chance, Osama disagreed with Arthur/Anwar and tried to put him in a bad light.

Each of these changes was a step toward disintegration.

When the week had passed, Ibrahim, with great apprehension, called the emergency number. A man answered. Ibrahim felt immediately relieved that it was not the deep voice that had spoken to him now several times.

"Hello? Who is calling?" this new voice said.

"It is Ibrahim al-Ryadi, Grandfather."

"And what is the problem?"

144

"We have not been able to reach Uncle in a week and a half, Grandfather, and our money has run out."

"I see. Why did you wait so long?"

"We were not sure if, perhaps, it was, it was, not yet an emergency."

"Hmmm. I will replenish your bank account."

"And what about Uncle?"

"I do not know. Goodbye."

"Goodbye."

Charles and Louise, listening in, were delighted. Other operatives in the Homeland Security Office had also recorded the call and the number it went to. Within a few minutes, they had identified "Grandfather" as Tariq Muhammad al-Mosuli, an Iraqi whom they knew had been close to Osama bin Laden. Now, they also had a recording of his voice. Subsequently, their devices also recorded an attempted call from al-Mosuli to Hassan's cell phone. No one answered, of course. In an hour, a transfer was authorized to the cell's bank in Amsterdam, and the agencies monitoring this account were able to trace the origin of the transfer to a bank in Riyadh. The name registered on the account was not Tariq Muhammad al-Mosuli, but the timing of the transfer made it clear that it was al-Mosuli who had authorized it. This gave the intelligence agencies at least another of his aliases. But the most important finding was the bank account itself. It had not been known to the agencies before, and it was very large.

They found their way into it and discovered many transfers to half a dozen accounts around the world. It seemed evident that they had discovered one of the main sources of funding for international terrorism. But they were puzzled by one thing. Transfers into al-Mosuli's account did not come from other banks. Indeed there were no transfers, only deposits marked with a bank code that they did not understand. Someone had established this account a long time ago with a very large deposit. This opening deposit, and several more of similar magnitude, were not bank transfers. At first, the agency assumed that these deposits came from the ancient underground system of money transfer, the *halawa*, and this was felt to be impenetrable. Consequently, no one tried very hard to understand it. When a new agent, fresh out of his training, was assigned the task of tracking down some loose ends, he came upon these transfers and realized that the deposits had not been coded as cash, as they would have if the money had arrived via the *halawa*. They had to be something else. Several different agencies in Washington then went to work to solve this mystery, for it was obvious that they were getting closer to understanding the source of some terrorists' funding.

Chapter 25
The American

Louise had been meeting with Arthur every day for several weeks, and the young man and older woman had formed a friendship, but it could not yet be called close. Nor was it one to which the two friends contributed equally. Louise wore her therapy hat, letting Arthur control the topics and pace of their conversations, although she never let on that she saw herself that way. Apparently, she'd succeeded in becoming a mother figure without his realizing it. He asked her opinions and sought her advice. He craved authority, but she hadn't provided it, afraid of scaring him off, but also to tease him into wanting more. But recently she'd decided to change.

She began by recalling some of the things she missed about America, but she balanced these comments with a few things she didn't like about the U.S. and things she liked about the Netherlands. She played a mothering role, but from a therapeutic perspective, and she kept her options open so that she could change direction if their relationship seemed to wander into territory not aligned with the more general mission.

"Remember the day we met?" she said.

"Yeah, sure."

"I was looking for decaf coffee."

"I remember."

"I still haven't found it."

"They just don't use it here, I guess."

"But why? If they're concerned about their own health, some people should have noticed that they sleep better without caffeine."

"I don't know."

"And smoking. How long is it going to take for them to realize that smoking is a killer?" Louise's face wrinkled up in acute puzzlement.

"That's weird, isn't it?" Arthur hated the smell of cigarette smoke, and had no difficulty agreeing with "Karen" on this point.

"Yes, it's weird. The research is unambiguous, and the Dutch people are literate, particularly in the scientific areas; they read new stories based on the research. They are keen on science. They must know that smoking causes emphysema and lung cancer."

"Heart disease too, doesn't it?" Arthur found himself caught up in the zeal of "Karen's" theme.

"Yes, and that's what I mean. You're an ordinary American guy, not some health geek. And you know that smoking is unhealthy." Calling him "an ordinary American guy" fit with Louise's plan perfectly, and she was glad to see that there was no negative reaction.

"So maybe they do know," Arthur said, playing devil's advocate.

"Maybe they don't care that much," she said, nodding her head as if she had reached an important conclusion.

She didn't expect an answer, and in fact she wanted him to sit with this idea for a while, so she terminated the conversation gently by announcing that she needed to be somewhere else, and they said goodbye for the day.

The idea that the Dutch cared less about their own health than Americans do was, in fact, a conclusion Louise had reached some time ago. It was hard to say, she felt, whether Americans were obsessed with health, or the Dutch (maybe Europeans generally) were overly casual about it. Or perhaps the Dutch character had a *soupçon*—they'd say "*een kleen beetje*"—of fatalism, an attitude that moved health concerns a few rungs down the ladder of importance. But the more she thought about it the more it seemed the other way around—that Americans were too concerned with their health, maybe because of the American emphasis on self-determination and self-reliance. What could be more self-reliant than wanting to control your own body in the face of a daily onslaught of microbes, carcinogens, antigens, and accidental injuries?

Even in the traffic regulations, and the driving behavior that resulted from them, this difference was visible. Americans drove more slowly and more carefully than the Dutch, and their laws were designed to prevent injury to driver, passenger, and pedestrian. The Dutch were more aggressive behind the wheel, almost the opposite of their personality when on foot or bicycle. The French were even worse in this way, and the Germans were extraordinarily incautious, even brash, on the road. For the Dutch, with their national pride placed so heavily on tolerance and decency, stepping out of their cars onto the sidewalks must involve a wrenching change in attitude from a careless assumption of raw power behind the wheel to deference, decency, and respect when on foot.

She intended to pursue this, and other differences between Americans and the Dutch, in her conversations with Arthur. She hoped only to raise his awareness of American character, values, traditions, and interests. She felt convinced that with enough of this increased awareness he would come to increasingly see himself as falling into the American categories and ultimately reconsider his loyalty as well. He was young and could change. But she knew it would not happen quickly.

In their next few meetings, he began to talk about his Muslim friends and told her that he had converted to Islam. She did not find this shocking, as he had thought she would. She simply accepted it as a part of who he was. It then became possible for her to ask him to compare Americans or the Dutch with Saudis or other Arabs he knew. In this way also, she hoped to raise his awareness of his own Americanness. She knew that her plan was beginning to work on the day that he began to complain about his Arabic friends. She listened attentively to these complaints, of which there were many, and she was careful never to say anything against the Arabs he complained about, knowing that he would have risen to their defense, and that this would have undermined the progress she had made with him.

This carefully contrived plan to win back the loyalty of Arthur was, after several weeks, making substantial headway. Louise had begun to talk about her home in Virginia and about qualities—of the people or of the land—in other parts of America that she thought Arthur might be attracted to. He seemed most attracted to New England—its structure, orderliness, education, and self-discipline. She did not mention California; she knew he would not go back there. So she tried to prepare him for a decision to return to a place where he would feel at home, but she knew the actual decision was a long way off, if it came at all.

She was just beginning to see that Arthur could actually turn, at least in his heart (the practicalities of abandoning the cell were still way too far away to be considered), when Henderson emailed them with a temporary change of assignment.

Chapter 26
The Diamonds

Analysis had led the Homeland Security people to conclude that the "Grandfather Account," as they called it in their discussions, must have been opened with a quantity of diamonds. Diamonds, the most valuable substance by weight, were the only way to quickly open a bank account as large as the Grandfather Account, and they knew it had been opened with one deposit. Also, some intelligence suggested that within the past few years the number of Arabic buyers of diamonds had increased, although they had nothing specific. But if diamonds had been used to open the account, there should be people in Belgium, particularly in Antwerp, who would know about it. Antwerp was the only place in the world where someone could discreetly buy several billion dollars' worth of diamonds.

Henderson's colleagues had suggested that Charles and Louise, already located in the Netherlands, could skip down to Belgium for a look-see, as they put it. See what the word on the street was. Charles and Louise rolled their eyes in unison as they heard this. Getting at information was always more difficult than the Washington folks realized. The Belgian diamond merchants had developed discreet methods, through well-established contacts in New York City, in South Africa, and more recently in Hong Kong, for many years. Their discretion was the cornerstone of their business, and Louise doubted she could hack into their computer records. Probably, she thought, their business would be conducted in cash. Records, if there were any, would be kept in pen and ink. If any records were computerized they would be protected by the most advanced security systems available, probably designed specifically for this one purpose.

They began researching the diamond business, from the African mines to the wholesalers in Antwerp and New York City, to large retailers in New York, Paris, London, and Berlin. The diamond wholesale business had been dominated for over a century by several families of Hasidic Jews. It had begun during the intense pogroms in Eastern Europe, when Jews realized their only defense against persecution was to accumulate secret wealth. Diamonds—valuable, small, and light in weight—could be hidden in clothing and transported with relative ease, to open accounts in foreign countries. This practice developed into a kind of underground economy -- secret, and separated from the national economies so that the value of the diamonds being transferred could not be influenced by economic fluctuations. Transportation was by courier, and records were often kept only by memory.

When the Holocaust descended on western Europe, the transfer of wealth to countries outside the reach of the Nazi horror helped many Jews escape. Establishing a bank account in England or the U.S. made their emigration to those countries possible. Unfortunately, these transfers were often not fast enough to allow escape from the Nazis.

Charles and Louise rented a car and drove the few hours to Antwerp. They decided to play the role of a wealthy American couple, looking to buy diamonds as a hedge against inflation. They dressed accordingly to reflect wealth of the American type. They could not hope to come anywhere near the kind of money that the Saudi would have had, but hoped that by pretending to be looking for several million dollars' worth of diamonds they could learn enough to confirm or deny the theory held by those in the Homeland Security Office. Henderson had some money— a very large sum for agents to have control of—sent by diplomatic pouch to the U.S. Consulate in Antwerp, so they could pick it up near where they would be showing it. They had no intention of buying any diamonds, but they needed to show that they had the money to do so, or they would not have been able to learn anything. They deposited the money in one of the Belgian banks, so that the diamond merchants could check it. In their cover story, they were simply exploring opinions. It gave them opportunities to talk with many different dealers. They spent a day doing this, just identifying the various dealers and trying to understand how someone with far more money than they had could convert it into diamonds. They dropped hints, from time to time, that they might be interested in a much larger transfer, and as a result were able to discover that it would be possible, although highly unusual, to buy the quantity the HS guys were thinking of.

Driving back to the Netherlands, through the southern part of Holland, they marveled at the clarity of the Dutch highway system, where the highway signs told drivers what cities to head for rather than what route numbers to take. Although it took some getting used to for the two Americans, it was actually easier to follow.

Charles was, in fact, contemplating this fact in his characteristically philosophical way when he thought of a way to verify the HS theory that diamonds had been used to open the accounts. He was thinking simply of the flow of traffic moving along the highway between Nijmegen and Den Bosch, and how the cars would have come from many points of origin to the first city, then for a while they would all be traveling along together. At Den Bosch, some would end their journey, others would then go on to other cities, all over northern Holland. Some would go to Germany or Denmark, a few even beyond to Poland or the Ukraine. Different as their ultimate destination was, they shared the characteristic of being between Nijmegen and Den Bosch for the same half-hour on this day. It was the idea of their having a shared characteristic at a certain point in time that gave him the idea for tracing the diamonds.

"For a deal of this size," he said to Louise, "the money and the diamonds have to all get together at the same time in Antwerp."

"Well," Louise was going to argue with the idea, "not all at once."

"OK, maybe over a period of a week."

"Yes, OK. You couldn't expect the purchaser to hang around forever."

"So the dealer—or maybe dealers—would have to have couriers bringing in diamonds from wherever they are—Durban, New York, whatever, to Antwerp. At the same time, they buyer would have to get all the money together in Antwerp at the same time."

"Does this transaction have to take place in Antwerp?"

"Not necessarily. But I'll bet the diamond dealers would want it to. Think of their own need for security."

"Let's look at the money first."

"OK. They would surely make wire transfers to pre-established accounts in every major bank in Antwerp, of which, if I am not mistaken, there are six."

"To total two billion dollars, they would have to transfer $166 million to each bank. It still seems like too much."

"I agree. If we included banks in Brussels, and Ghent, then also Lille in France, and Maastricht in Holland, maybe some other cities, the amounts could be reduced to a couple of million for each bank."

"They would need probably three people to visit all these banks, make the withdrawals, and deliver them to Antwerp. It could be done in several days. One person could do it in a week."

"So that's doable. What about the diamonds?"

"That's a little more difficult because of the distances, but I think 20 couriers, each making three trips, could bring $2 billion worth of diamonds together in a week."

"Are there enough diamonds in the world to do it?"

"Yes, but it would seriously drop the supply. And that would cause a spike in prices."

"Good. That's another thing we can look for."

"What I was thinking before about traffic was that a look at all the airline reservations during successive weeks should show a pattern of increased tickets purchased for flights to Antwerp. The increase would be small, but maybe it could be detected."

"Yes, I can do that. It's just a little program. I can vary the time window too," said Louise, as the excitement of the project catching her imagination.

"OK then. When we get back you can do that."

Later, in Amsterdam, Louise wrote the program to begin examining one-week windows, starting from the date the deposit was made in Riyadh and working backward. She found a spike in tickets to Antwerp sold just one week earlier, which was very promising. But they needed to confirm it with a flow of money out of Belgium and probably French and Dutch banks, during the same time. They could not get such a quantity of information by hacking, so they had Henderson set the process going with international law enforcement. The French decided not to cooperate, but the Dutch and Belgian authorities permitted an investigation of the patterns, although they balked at allowing access to actual accounts. They would not reveal the identities of the individuals involved, but they would themselves seek information from the banks about withdrawals made during the week being investigated.

Sure enough, there they were, a series of large withdrawals made during the same week that so many airplane tickets to Antwerp were used. With this information, the police were then willing to order the banks to reveal the identities of those who had access to the accounts, and they found that the withdrawals were all made by men with Saudi passports. These identifications were false, and the accounts had been closed out with the withdrawals, but they were able to determine the banks from which these Dutch and Belgian accounts were set up: only a few of them, all in Arabic countries. The bulk of the money had come from Saudi Arabia and Pakistan, and establishing the identification of the people who had opened these accounts would be a major step forward in tracking down the funding of terrorist groups—although the authorities would need the cooperation of the Saudis and other governments to do so, and this would take time and diplomacy. Nevertheless, they had made some major progress and wrote a report to Washington that was well received.

***

Charles and Louise congratulated themselves briefly for a little side project well done. Then they got back to work on the Amsterdam cell. Charles had an idea which he hoped might trigger an actual breakdown of the cell. It was an elaborate ruse, which had to be set up over a period of time.

With the help of an Arabic scholar in Washington he composed a letter, addressed to Ibrahim, written in the flowery ancient language of the Holy Qur'an and copied onto an authentic-looking piece of parchment. The Arabic script was carefully executed to resemble Qur'anic writing. The text of the letter was as follows:

Dear Ibrahim:

I have given thee warnings. I have punished thee for thy sinfulness. I have shown thee where in Holy Qur'an the Prophet says that a man of peace is to be admired. Sometimes, Ibrahim, violence is necessary, but not often, and it is not your way, Ibrahim. Be my prophet, Ibrahim. Tell my people that they can find the land they dream of through peace. Tell them, Ibrahim.

The parchment was a synthetic material that would degrade rapidly on exposure to air, leaving only a kind of dust. It was then wrapped in carefully tanned goatskin, and the goatskin was dipped in red wax. The wax kept out the air that would degrade the parchment, and the goatskin protected the parchment from the wax. The whole package, however, had an ancient look to it. Charles had this package sent by diplomatic pouch to the embassy in Riyadh, and an attaché wrapped it in brown paper, addressed it to Ibrahim al-Ryadi at the woonboot address in Amsterdam, then drove with it to Mecca, the holiest city of Islam, located in Saudi Arabia. There, the attaché had it mailed, postmarked with the stamp of Mecca, guaranteeing with a hefty bribe that it would not be opened, and declaring on the customs form that it was a "letter." When it arrived in the Netherlands, it was immediately considered suspicious because of its weight and origin, and a bomb squad dressed in biohazard suits x-rayed it to see the letter. Finding nothing suspicious, they rewrapped it and sent it on its way. It was delivered to Ibrahim the following day.

At the bottom of the letter was a small mark that resembled an Arabic character, but it was not a character that actually existed. It was a new shape. Ibrahim stared at it for a long time but could not make it out. He showed the letter to his cousin, and it was good that he did because within two days it had disintegrated, the letters fading, and the parchment-like material falling apart. His cousins were puzzled, and he told them about the cell phone calls he had received. They were skeptical, but they didn't entirely dismiss the idea that the calls and the letter were of divine origin. They thought about the "punishments," and particularly about the long bout of "food poisoning" they had all had. They thought about Osama's peculiar behavior, and about the terrible job they had done during the dry run. They began to wonder if perhaps they were not meant to be a terrorist cell.

Chapter 27
The Emigrant

"We have money!" Ibrahim shouted down the hatch as he arrived at the woonboot from the bank.

"Excellent!" said Arthur/Anwar, who was closest to him.

"We can pay our bills," said Akhmed, who had that particular job.

Muhammad smiled, suppressing a giggle. In fact, all of the woonboot occupants were feeling more optimistic. Their money was coming from a different account, but they did not know this. Soon they would acquire a new "uncle," but this would take a while, and meanwhile it seemed as though life in the woonboot had returned to a more jovial, a more youthful, atmosphere. It would have spoiled their mood to know that the leaders of Al Qaeda, disappointed and dispirited with the outcome of the cell's dry run, which had resulted in one of their main operatives being arrested, were considering cutting them off completely from the parent organization.

They returned to their daily routine: classes at the university, weekly shopping, study or television in the evenings. The only difference was that Ibrahim kept raising the idea, subtly and vaguely to be sure, that perhaps they should abandon their connection with Al Qaeda. This idea did not fall on deaf ears.

Akhmed, for one, welcomed the possibility of the cell's breaking up. A breakup should enable him to pursue more energetically, and more honestly, his courtship of Takhmina. As a first step, he called the Immigration Office of the Dutch government. They gave him an appointment time for the next day, much more quickly than he had anticipated, and he went in, a feeling of light-heartedness coursing through his veins. In spite of the renewed optimism in the woonboot, Akhmed now saw the possibility of another way, and it filled him with joy.

As he approached the building, however, he was nervous. He had been engaged in subversive activity, and he did not want the authorities to know about it. He looked up. Could this be the right address? The building was cubic in shape but designed to look as though it was resting atilt on one corner. Furthermore, it was not square to the street, and set back on an open area. The front of the building was a bright red, but the side that Akhmed could see was yellow. It looked like a child's toy block, and in fact the building had originally been designed as an elementary school. The population had shifted in this area of the city, and now there were not enough children to sustain a school, so the building had been sold to the government, which had installed the Office of Immigration in it.

Akhmed entered very cautiously. It was hard for him to be sure that the building would be sturdy. Inside, the floor was level, which was a surprise, judging from the outside appearance. But the walls were painted in bright, primary colors, and there were fingerpaintings and other works of art by children decorating the walls. The new occupants had been tickled by the juvenile architecture and decided to preserve the childlike flavor of the building. The Dutch people love children, and they love even more the idea of childhood, of freedom from responsibility, giddiness, nonchalance, and play. Probably they treasure these characteristics of childhood precisely because they approach adult life with intense seriousness and obsessive responsibility. By letting the building retain the influence of its former small occupants, they gave themselves a smile when they came in to work. There were many of these remains of the children: signs to the various departments in large block letters and bright colors, the artwork on the wall, the bathroom signs that said *jongens* and *meisjes*—boys and girls—instead of men and women. Akhmed was disturbed by this juvenile interior decorating; he thought it was inappropriate for a government building. But he dutifully followed the big block-letter signs to the Applications Office, where he was to have his interview.

This room was more serious. The only wall decorations were some modern abstract weavings, and not many of those. They were only barely appropriate, but better than the silliness in the hallway decorations. He sat in a small room with a number of other people in loose chairs facing a row of glass enclosures. In each little glass box sat one of the interviewers. "It is like the red light district," he said to himself. This thought—suggesting adulthood—might have put him at ease, but it did not. He wanted his application to be taken seriously, and it was hard for him to believe that this would happen in such a place.

"Elganayin, number six," a bodyless voice announced in the cheery Dutch accent that seemed always to be used for public announcements. A green light began to blink over one of the glass booths. A dark young man rose from the front row of chairs, walked to one of the glass booths and went inside. The green light stopped blinking. A few minutes went by.

"Lin-soo, number four," the voice announced, as another green light began to blink. An Asian girl got up, her head lowered modestly, and entered the appropriate booth.

Akhmed looked around. There were only two other people in the room. He would not have long to wait. Minutes passed by, and his nervousness grew. He watched as two other applicants were called. One looked like a Turkish man. The other was somewhat Asian looking, Mongol perhaps—Akhmed couldn't be sure. Guessing the nationalities of the applicants was not entertaining enough to keep his anxiety at bay.

"Al-Ryadi, number one," he heard, and he looked up and saw the blinking illuminated number 1. He left his chair and went in.

The applications officer was a young man, about Akhmed's age, which surprised him. He had expected somebody older and more authoritative. The young man was blonde and blue-eyed with ruddy cheeks.

"I am Akhmed al-Ryadi," he said in his best Dutch.

The young officer extended his hand and announced his name, but it didn't register in Akhmed's mind. The Dutch names often sounded similar to him. They all began with "von," or "fun" as the Dutch pronounced it, and then went off into other peculiar sounds. He realized that he had forgotten the man's name as soon as he heard it and wondered if he would have to know it later. His palms were moist by this time.

At the interview, he exaggerated a little, telling the Immigration officer that he was interested in staying in the Netherlands to complete his studies and then perhaps to become a citizen, if they would have him. His current predicament, however, was that his money was going to run out. He had carefully rehearsed this presentation, looking up some of the words he was unsure of.

"My parents have been supporting me, but they have fallen on difficult financial times and cannot do so any more. Is there anything that I can do to stay here?" He managed the Dutch fairly well, and he asked with an earnestness that was fueled by his feelings for Takhmina.

"Yes, of course. I see that you are learning to speak Dutch. It is a difficult language, isn't it?"

"It is difficult for me. It is very different from Arabic."

"Yes, I am sure that it is." The official had been gathering papers together in front of him, pulling one from one bin off to his right, then another from another bin off to his left, and assembling them on the desk in front of him as he spoke to Akhmed. "Here is what you need to do. First, you will need to fill out this form." His finger landed with practiced accuracy on the title of one of the papers. "By submitting this form, you will be requesting that your status be changed from that of a visiting student to a landed immigrant."

The Dutch word for "landed immigrant" was not in Akhmed's vocabulary yet, although it soon would be, and he worried momentarily.

"You will then need to have an interview," the officer went on, "possibly a series of interviews, with the Immigration officials. They will be impressed, I think, with your ability to speak Dutch. If these interviews work out well, your application will be approved. Once you are a landed immigrant, you will be eligible to receive a student stipend. It is really not as difficult as it sounds, much easier than in Germany." The official smiled warmly at the comparison as he handed the papers to Akhmed. He enjoyed feeling superior to Germans, although the sentiment was completely lost on Akhmed.

The warm smile was culturally alien to Akhmed. In Saudi Arabia such a smile might mean that you were about to be arrested or struck. It would not have been friendly. It took much effort for Akhmed to keep himself from cringing from the blow he expected.

On the top of the papers the officer put a business card with his name on it. "If you have any questions, call me." He smiled again and gestured with his hand toward the waiting room, signaling that the interview was over. Akhmed was glad to be out from the brothel-like interview room and out of the bizarre building. Outside, he could breathe more easily. Apparently, he had done well.

Akhmed took the form to a café where he ordered a cup of tea and sat down at one of the tables to fill out the form. The tea calmed him, and in retrospect he did not think his initial contact with the Dutch government had gone badly. He was encouraged.

He took the filled-out papers back to the strange building the same day, followed the childish signs to the right office, and submitted his form. Then he called Takhmina.

"I have applied for Dutch citizenship," he told her enthusiastically.

"Was the interview difficult?" she asked.

"No, not at all. But I will have to go back for another interview, perhaps two more, and these will be more difficult."

"Good luck," she said, "I hope you make it."

He went back to the woonboot feeling quite lighthearted. Lately, he noticed, aside from his anxieties over contact with the Dutch government, he was much happier than he had been. He attributed this change to Takhmina, although in a corner of his mind he realized that some of his happiness came from the fact that he would not be setting off a bomb at the World Court.

When he got home he did not tell his brothers or Ibrahim what he had done. Akhmed was by nature honest and forthright, and he had recently engaged in more deception than he could ever have imagined. He was deceiving Takhmina about the cell. Of course, he had to do that. He was deceiving his brothers and cousin about his relationship with Takhmina, and he was deceiving them also about his intentions with regard to the cell. Now, he was deceiving the government of the Netherlands to the extent that they would be supporting him. It all made him feel queasy, but the queasiness was trumped by the sense of new possibilities and freedoms.

Chapter 28
The Changes

Arthur too listened to Ibrahim's preaching and even agreed with some of the ideas, but he was not fully convinced. He said nothing to the others. He believed that if the other cell members felt that he was drifting away from his jihadist convictions, his American origins would lead them to question his loyalty. Besides, he was not yet convinced that he should leave Al Qaeda. He was just confused.

In the last few weeks he'd had vivid dreams about living in America. In the dreams, he held different jobs: a businessman, a craftsman, a plumber or electrician. In the dreams, he saw himself working hard, getting up early, applying himself with dedication to his occupation and becoming successful. His dreams were always bathed in sunlight, golden and warm, like the air in the spring. Trees leafed out and grass grew underfoot. They were beautiful dreams, and he woke from them with regret. He told Louise/Karen about them. She listened, asked questions about details, and made no judgment or interpretation, which helped him see them as his creations—expressions of how he felt at this point in his life.

"Your attitudes are changing. You are growing, as everyone does," she said softly, hoping he would accept the idea, but knowing how difficult it was because he'd long armored himself with a coat of fixed beliefs.

"But I, I, well, I am not sure if I really want the life that I see in these dreams," Arthur said with uncertainty.

"You don't have to be sure," Louise said, looking directly into his eyes. "Not now. Now, you only have feelings. Just let yourself feel them. It isn't necessary to make decisions."

"But if I feel this way, I am not being true to my beliefs," Arthur said, his voice trembling slightly, unsure but deeply affected by the closeness he felt toward her.

"The dreams express how you feel, not things that you are doing. You cannot help but be true to your beliefs. You will always be true to them, whatever they are, even as they change. There is no right or wrong about feelings; they just are whatever they are. They are a part of you, like the color of your skin or of your eyes. There is no reason to feel ashamed about any of them, past or future." Louise delivered these last few phrases with passion. They were part of *her* belief. She almost checked herself, but realized that Arthur would take her excitement as a part of her feelings for him, which he'd seen her express before, like the mother he'd never really had. She took his hand and wished him well, excusing herself from their conversation with gentleness. He accepted this kind of physical expression from her now; it seemed natural to him. His need to have this kind of relationship made it easier for him to accept her touching and the gentle tone of her voice. He had come a long way.

Arthur always left his meetings with Karen feeling better than he did when they began. He didn't understand why this should be so, but he didn't fight it. After this most recent conversation he felt freer than ever, as if he could do or be anything. He felt that Allah had sent Karen to him to help him find his way.

The others too were changing.

Of all the Saudis in the cell, Muhammad was the most moved by Ibrahim's pronouncements and references to the Holy Qur'an. From the beginning, his attachment to the group had been based more on his family connection to the other Saudis than to any deep conviction. And now, when Ibrahim spoke of the need to follow the teaching of the Holy Qur'an, and mentioned specific passages that talked of peace among men and of God's hatred for war, Muhammad listened and believed.

166

It helped enormously, of course, that he was by nature the most peaceful of the men. He had not been hurt as much as the others in the first place, and consequently had not accepted with as much fervor the preaching of the madras mullahs. He was always just going along. It was a relief to hear Ibrahim talk of peace. There had always been tension in the woonboot; they were planning for a violent act. As it became less likely that they would carry out the bombing, Muhammad's anxiety about it evaporated like street puddles in the sun. If the cell broke up, he would stay with one of his brothers and be comfortable with himself and with the world.

Osama was still angry with his brothers, but less so with Ibrahim. Ibrahim had already concluded that Osama's odd behavior, which had almost disappeared, was a result of Allah's very specific intervention and therefore not Osama's fault. As a result, he saw Osama not as some crazy person, but as an instrument of God. So, he did not discount Osama's opinions the way that Akhmed and Muhammad did. He listened to Osama with an attentiveness that was strikingly different from that of his brothers, who were apt, when Osama was speaking, to leave the room to go to the bathroom or get a snack from the refrigerator. Osama's feelings toward Ibrahim were therefore much more loving. With his brothers, Osama was angry. With Ibrahim, he felt accepted and worthy.

Osama was not convinced that the letter Ibrahim received was authentic. In fact, none of the cell members were as sure of it as Ibrahim. Osama, more than the others, had lost confidence in his ability to carry out an attack. He felt out of control—as if someone else was running him. Had they been asked to attack, he might have run away, afraid that he would fail. It was more for this personal reason than for religious ones that he listened to Ibrahim's vague suggestions.

Chapter 29
The High

Charles and Louise decided on one more intervention into the cell. They were not sure what the effect would be, but they felt it could not harm their cause and might be helpful.

Once again, they opened the trunk of the car during the three-minute interval. This time, Charles leaned down and sniffed the groceries, scooping the air above them toward his nose with a cupped hand. He recognized what he was looking for and reached down into one of the bags and removed a box of oatmeal raisin cookies. He knew it would be there from his continued monitoring of their garbage. It was a snack they all liked, and they usually bought two boxes. Charles took both. They closed the trunk and walked away.

After the groceries were all bought into the woonboot, there were immediate complaints from the cell members.

"Where are the oatmeal cookies? We agreed on two boxes."

"I do not know," said Osama, who had done the shopping that week. "I know I bought them. I remember putting them in the cart."

"You probably left them there," said Akhmed with very little kindness in his voice.

Osama went back to the store to complain.

"Yes, *mineer*, of course. They were probably not packed. Let me get you two boxes."

And while Osama waited, the store owner went to the shelf and brought back two boxes of oatmeal cookies, figuring that they had not been packed and had then been returned to the shelf—or perhaps stolen—before Osama discovered the loss. He recognized the Arab as a regular customer and wanted to please him.

When Osama returned to the woonboot, his failure to do even the simplest task, the food shopping, was almost forgiven.

Louise and Charles then spent the week baking batch after batch of oatmeal cookies, until they had achieved a good replica with regard to flavor, aroma and appearance of the original. They then baked a final batch spiked with the marijuana that was so easy to obtain in Amsterdam, carefully packed them in the original packages, sealed them by pressing the wax impregnated paper together while they blew on it with a hair dryer. They told Henderson to tell the agent running Talgat to warn him that the oatmeal cookies would be spiked.

On the next Monday they opened the trunk during the three-minute interval, substituted the spiked cookies for the two boxes that had just been bought and were back in their apartment across the street before the second load was brought in. They had been very careful to keep the dose light, and had tested the marijuana they bought for potency, then followed directions that Henderson had obtained from the Washington experts about how much to include it in the recipe. They wanted the group to get high, but not suspicious.

The result was an evening of laughter and fun. Arthur was the only one who thought they'd been dosed with marijuana, indeed he knew the feeling well and recognized it, but he figured it was just one of the other cell members, probably Muhammad, the jokester, having fun with the group. He simply enjoyed the experience.

The next week, following the suggestion of one of Henderson's colleagues in the State Department, they dosed one of the milk cartons with a marijuana liquid derivative, from one of the Amsterdam head shops. They bought a carton of milk that matched the kind the cell members used and carefully injected the drug into the carton with a hypodermic needle, puncturing the carton at one of the top seams, which they then resealed. It was easy matter to substitute the dosed carton for one that had just been bought during the window of opportunity between the loads of groceries.

This time, the woonboot was filled with hilarity at breakfast, and they all went off to the university a little high. On the whole, they had come down by the time lectures started. Charles and Louise dosed them in this way four different times, changing the food product each time. Each time the result was the same, an hour or two of laughter, and then a gradual return to normality. They told Henderson each time to warn Talgat.

During one of these party-like times, when anything anyone said that was the least bit different struck them all as hilarious, Ibrahim with no warning at all said "We don't need no fucking bomb." At the moment it was the funniest thing imaginable, and they all took up the chorus of "We don't need no fucking bomb," dragging out the word "bomb" at the end. They stood up in twos and threes, dancing like chorus girls while they chanted the line for a few seconds then collapsing on the floor or sofa, helpless with laughter. And even though the sentiment had been voiced at a time when they did not feel any restraints on their behavior, the thought stayed with them when the restraints returned, like the lingering feeling of happiness after a beautiful dream.

But when they thought seriously about abandoning their goal of setting off a bomb at the World Court, which meant also severing their ties with Al Qaeda, the thoughts were stopped by some practical barriers. What would they do for money? Where would they go? What would Al Qaeda do? They believed that Al Qaeda might come looking for them, and might well kill them if they were found. Their training had not included threats of the consequences of disloyalty.

In fact, there was no such danger. The organization limited the knowledge of each cell, so that their capture or defection would have little effect on the organization as a whole. They didn't know their superiors, and they knew no other cells, except for the necessary contacts for getting the bomb components together, and even that was restricted. None of the components was actually stored at the pick-up locations; they were brought there by those cell members on the day they were signaled for, and only the person transporting them knew the location where they were stored. Most cells lacked even these contacts; the members had to find or manufacture their own bomb components if bombing was their mission. But the Amsterdam group was young and not entirely trustworthy, an opinion the leaders formed during training based on the lack of fervor in Muhammad's attitude, and the foreignness of Arthur/Anwar and to a certain extent also of Talgat. It would not be difficult for the leaders simply to abandon them.

So, although the cell members had not yet begun to speak of it among themselves, except when they were high, each was thinking in his own mind about how to get away and how to get money. It was not an easy time for any of them.

Chapter 30
The Entrepreneur

It was easiest for Arthur to figure out how to extricate himself, although he suffered agonies of conscience over the rightness of his actions. He had mentioned money several times to Louise, so she had a good idea of what his intentions were and that money was the obstacle to fulfilling them.

"There is a good way for you to make some money," she offered at one of their meetings after he had complained again about not having enough funds.

"What is that?" he asked with his characteristic intensity.

"There is a big demand for tutors in English," she said.

"I don't know how to teach English. I just speak it." Arthur smiled at his little joke, and Louise felt a surge of delight at how normal he appeared at times. It was as if she could see his jihadist intensity unraveling in strands before her eyes.

"Many people have learned the language, but they want to practice talking with a native speaker. That would be you."

"What would we talk about?" he asked.

"It doesn't matter at all. Talk about what they want to talk about." Louise shrugged her shoulders while looking into Arthur's pale eyes.

"And how much would they pay me?"

"I don't know exactly, but you can find out easily enough at the University. I have seen notices on the student message boards asking for native English speakers to practice conversational skills." She leaned back in her chair, relaxing, to show him how easy it would be.

"I could probably do that," he said.

"Of course you could. The people who want to practice will be from Turkey, Africa, Iran. I'm sure they have a lot to talk about. You might even enjoy it," she added as an afterthought.

Arthur smiled. When he left Louise that day, he had a plan, and any plan contains optimism, something Arthur hadn't felt for a long time. He went to the University and examined the message boards. There were several requests for conversation practice, and he tore off the little slips of paper with the telephone numbers. He made several calls, arranging appointments with students who were, just as "Karen" had said, from all over the world and eager to practice speaking English. He and his new clients agreed upon hourly rates. Arthur knew not to ask too much. The clientele was not wealthy. But each hour he spent talking with these refugees would add to the money he received from Ibrahim. He opened a savings account. With a little extra effort, and without anyone knowing about it, he would be able to accumulate enough money for a plane ticket to America and some money to get an apartment and support himself while he looked for a job. He saw himself doing this in Vermont, which had become for him a kind of paradise. He was beginning to think of it as a real possibility.

Akhmed and Takhmina had already talked about other countries. Akhmed's idea of becoming a Dutch citizen while she finished her studies was one idea. It had the advantage, and it was a big advantage from Akhmed's point of view, of allowing them to see each other while she finished her premed major. She had only a year to go. After that, medical school in Denmark or Sweden was appealing, but they would have to learn yet another language, and they were already tired from learning Dutch. Canada seemed like a better choice: They could speak English, and the coursework they found on the internet in both medicine and business at the Canadian universities seemed excellent. The big question was timing.

Although the Immigration officer he had spoken to had been most welcoming, Akhmed had been a little put off by his manner and by the strange building. After he had submitted his application, he began to worry once again. What if they knew about the cell? He did not think he would be arrested. If they'd wanted to arrest him, they would already have done so. He would probably not be allowed to become a Dutch citizen, not if they thought he was going to do something violent. He wished he hadn't been so hasty in applying.

These worries grew, and he decided to get out of the Netherlands as soon as possible. It wasn't just the Dutch government he was worried about. He was also frightened of retribution by Al Qaeda. Unable to share these worries with Takhmina or his brothers he had them all to himself, and they kept growing.

Leaving the country would mean leaving the University without a degree. He gave up the idea of becoming a landed immigrant in the Netherlands. Even if the Dutch authorities did not know about the cell, he would always be worried about Al Qaeda finding him. He would have to transfer the credits he'd earned to a university in Canada, but admissions officers from several Canadian universities assured him that transfer would not be a problem. The Dutch university was well respected throughout the world and any work he completed successfully in the Netherlands would be honored in Canada.

Takhmina, however, had different ideas.

"But I don't want to go to Canada. Not now, anyway. I want to stay here and finish my degree," she said to Akhmed. Takhmina balked at the idea of transferring to another university, particularly when it was to follow a "boy"— she always thought of Akhmed as a boy. It would look bad in her record, diminishing the appearance of steadfast purpose. She was in fact steadfast and didn't like giving up on something she'd begun.

Akhmed was not used to having women oppose his wishes, but he was so smitten with Takhmina that he decided her plain speech was a good thing. It meant that they were a modern, western couple, and that fit comfortably with the sense of freedom that he'd come to treasure.

He couldn't tell her why he wanted to leave the Netherlands.

They were sitting in the university cafeteria, several levels below the street level, having coffee during a break from classes. They'd been meeting like this almost every day.

Takhmina put her coffee cup down and tightened the clip that held her hair in place.

"What's your hurry to leave?"

"I want to get started on my education in business. My, uh, my English is good enough now," he answered, looking at her and for a moment losing his train of thought in the darkness of her eyes.

She had come to recognize these moments when Akhmed's feelings for her seemed to destroy his thought process. She had an image of his brain crackling with something like static electricity creating little short circuits in the transmission of clear and logical thought. She liked having the power to make Akhmed's brain disintegrate into bursts of static electricity, even though the result was a befuddlement that was not particularly appealing. In the end, she was not convinced by his arguments about why he wanted to go to Canada. But when he reached across the table and took her hand and looked into her eyes, she felt something that she had not felt before, something which she had pushed down deep inside her so that she could pursue her education single mindedly. If she had not lost her own focus so totally at this moment, she might have smelled the ozone of her own brain's random static.

"I want to marry you," he said, his voice husky with feeling.

"Oh," she said, startled at the feelings that suddenly coursed through her body.

"I will make money first," he began. "Then I will go to Canada and enroll in business courses."

Takhmina's eyes were misting over.

"When you have finished your university degree, you can join me, and we can marry in Canada. We will be Canadian citizens. It is a beautiful country, with friendly people and freedom."

"Why can't you stay here and we can finish our degrees together?" she asked.

"I do not want to stay in the Netherlands any longer than possible," he said. "If I go to Canada first, I can have everything ready for us—a place to live, a job. I will know what you must do when you come. It will work."

"Yes," she said. "Yes. I will marry you and live in Canada." She gulped a little at what she was saying. "But I am still going to be a doctor."

"Of course," he assured her. "I want that for you also."

He had not really planned on asking her to marry him. He knew that he did not have the money necessary to send a bride price to her parents. It was another reason for his going to Canada, where he believed he would be able to make more money, although he didn't tell her that.

Takhmina received money from her parents in Jordan, who would have gladly subsidized her travel to Canada to go to medical school there, but they wouldn't subsidize Akhmed's travel, with or without Takhmina. So Akhmed had to figure out some way of making enough money in the Netherlands to get himself to Canada.

He did have an entrepreneurial spirit, and he devised a scheme that worked. With a beginning stake of $100, which Takhmina lent him, he bought four tickets to an upcoming rock concert. The concert sold out as most of them did, and on the evening of the event, Akhmed stationed himself outside the concert hall and sold all four tickets for $100 each. He then paid Takhmina back and waited for the next event, investing his profit of $300 in the same way. Folk music concerts, plays, even classical music concerts at the world-famous *Concertgebouw* were likely to sell out, and Akhmed quickly became an expert scalper. In a couple of months, and with a very small expenditure of time, he had saved up several thousand dollars, had applied and been accepted at a Canadian university, and obtained a Canadian visa. At the Canadian university, he could finish his undergraduate education and then go on for an MBA. He felt guilty abandoning his brothers, but circumstances warranted it and it was a natural way for life to proceed when he had a prospective bride. Also, he hoped that someday he and his brothers would be reunited in his new homeland.

Ibrahim did not have the same money problems that the others did. His problem was his conscience. As the leader of the cell, he had access to the bank account, and the amount that was deposited there was adequate to stake him for a trip to Istanbul, where he could practice the religion that had become so important to him. He would have liked to return to Saudi Arabia, and perhaps someday he would be able to, preaching a gospel of nonviolence. At this moment, such a gospel would be unpopular, and it would call such attention to himself that he would likely not survive. So, Istanbul had seemed like a place he could disappear into, find an Arabic-speaking community, get a simple job, and become invisible for a while.

As he pondered this plan, while sitting alone in the mosque, he could not figure out how to make it work. He would have to leave the other cell members in the lurch. He had no qualms about abandoning Talgat and Anwar, but he could not abandon his cousins, for whom he felt a paternal responsibility. Of course, he didn't know of Akhmed's plans. And there was not enough money deposited in the bank account each month to fly all four of them to Istanbul and keep them alive long enough to find jobs. There was, in fact, not quite enough even for the airfare.

So, it was with some misgivings but with great faith in the strength of family ties that he arranged a meeting of the four al-Ryadis and asked them to keep it secret from Anwar and Talgat.

Chapter 31
The Breakup

They met at a café on *Oranjestraat*, not far from the Central Station. It was noisy in the café. A throng of students were drinking beer and talking in loud voices about politics, culture, language, and their own futures. The chaotic background did not hinder the intense discussion of the Saudis.

Ibrahim came right to the point. "I propose that we all abandon this madness with the bomb. It is not the will of Allah. We do not do it very well anyway, and I think maybe Allah makes us bad at it because He does not want us to do it."

The others were not surprised to hear Ibrahim talk this way, and they were all feeling a new sense of happiness and freedom, in spite of their connection to Al Qaeda, because of the fun they'd been having in the woonboot. They didn't suspect that they were being given light doses of drugs; they knew only that for a few hours they felt a wonderful sense of freedom, and then, when they later went about their everyday business, the heavy presence of Al Qaeda and their difficult and tension-filled mission was oppressing. The contrast was powerful.

No one was more surprised than Ibrahim to find that they all agreed immediately. He had expected resistance to his idea. Instead, they were right on board. His earlier hints that Allah might disapprove of what they were doing had been completely sincere, and paved the way for the acceptance of the more direct statement he made today.

Ibrahim then brought up the problem of money.

"How can we pay for the costs of separating from our Uncle?" he asked.

Akhmed cleared his throat. "My brothers, and my good cousin Ibrahim," he began, and they all knew that he would say something important. He began nervously, holding his hands tightly together on the tabletop.

"I think I can help you with the problem of money." His hesitancy suggested that they shouldn't celebrate yet.

"I have met a girl, a Jordanian, and we are beginning to plan a future together." There were smiles at this from Osama and Muhammad, but Ibrahim's brow immediately wrinkled.

"What is she like?" Ibrahim asked. "And her parents. What do they think? You cannot pay a bride price." He saw a number of possible objections to Akhmed's plans, but the last one, the bride price was more than a possibility; it was a deal-breaker.

"No, certainly not yet. We have only recently spoken of marriage. Her parents are very wealthy and would surely object to me now. But I hope to better myself and be able to pay the bride price."

"But," said Ibrahim, "if her parents are wealthy, it will be very expensive, unless..." he hesitated. "She is not ... deformed, ugly perhaps, or ..." he hesitated again. "She is not ...," and he used an Arabic word that meant "soiled," a word used to describe dirty laundry.

"No," said Akhmed. "She is not soiled. She is a virgin. She is pretty and very smart and wants to become a doctor."

They all looked concerned, Ibrahim most of all. For him, a woman who wanted to become educated was almost as bad as one who was "soiled." But, although it diminished her in their eyes as a prospective bride for their brother and cousin, it was not unthinkable for any of them. They had been exposed to western customs in the Netherlands, and they had seen many women being educated, many of them outpacing their male classmates. For Osama and Muhammad, the idea of their brother marrying such a woman seemed a little sad, because they felt that they would lose him as a brother, but they could easily imagine that he could be happy. Ibrahim, however, thought happiness would elude Akhmed.

"I am planning to go to Canada," said Akhmed, plunging into the most difficult part of what he had to tell them. "I have already made quite a lot of money to fund this trip, and I can help you to do the same."

He went on. "I have spoken with a Canadian Immigration official. We can become landed immigrants." "But what if we are identified as criminals?" asked Osama.

"We can change our names and adopt new identities," he countered.

They were dismayed to hear about his intention to go to Canada, but the mention of a solution to the money problem and the legal means to stay in Holland powerfully mitigated their worries about the future. He explained about scalping tickets, and they saw immediately how it could work. With all of them doing it, and by using some of their living allowance they could buy up a substantial block of tickets. They could even travel to other cities and scalp tickets there. There were risks—bad weather, a cancellation, even last-minute bad publicity might leave them holding a lot of worthless tickets. So, they put together a plan, which included diversification among different performances, various Dutch and Belgian cities, and some caution in the number of tickets they bought. They also were aware that scalping was illegal in Belgium and the Netherlands, and they had to be careful to make their sales surreptitiously.

Within a few weeks, however, they had worked a rock concert with an American band and made a lot of money.

"Look at this!" Osama said, flashing a wad of euros.

"Yes, and there will be more," said Akhmed.

"I too have done quite well, thanks be to Allah," said Ibrahim.

"Soon we will have enough for all of our plans," said Muhammad.

"If Allah wills it," added Ibrahim in the traditional Muslim hope for the future.

Osama and Muhammad began to look for someone who could create false documents for them before they talked to Immigration and filled out forms. As international terrorists, this should not have been difficult for them, but they were not trained in tactics of this sort, and they could not ask for help from Al Qaeda. But they made inquiries among the many foreign students at the university. It did not take long for them to get the contact information for someone who could supply false papers.

They went to the address, which was a souvenir shop in the central part of Amsterdam. They had been told to ask for "Henri."

"Monsieur Henri is in there," the store clerk pointed to a door at the back of the store.

They went through the door, their hearts beating rapidly. Terrorists or not, it was the first genuinely illegal thing they had done in Amsterdam, and they were worried. "Henri" sat behind a small desk, surrounded by books and papers. He was a middle-aged man of indeterminate ethnicity. His face was round, and his double chins wobbled as he moved his head, which was partially covered with straight dark hair. He wore half spectacles over which he peered at them, looking somewhat like a turtle. He could have been an accountant.

"We need passports, visa, a whole new identity," said Osama, suppressing a giggle. Muhammad looked at him and nodded in agreement. They both held their breaths.

"Of course. I can do this. Do you want a driver's license also?"

"That won't be necessary, just the minimum to change our names and disappear."

"I see," said "Henri" in a voice that was a little bored. "It will cost 500 euros for each document. What passport do you want?"

"What is best, do you think?"

"Probably the European passport. There are so many different nationalities that your appearance will not arouse suspicion. Also, with the European passport you can travel to many different places without needing a visa."

"So that will be only 500 euros."

"No, the European passport costs 1000 euros, but it is worth it."

"OK," they agreed. "We will give you 500 now and 500 more when it is done." They gave him money.

"What names do you want to use?"

They decided to keep their first names—they were very common names in any case—and simply change their last names to something equally Arabic. In a week, they had new identities and were poorer by an additional 500 euros, although with their newfound wealth it did not seem like much. They found an apartment in an area just outside the city.

Meanwhile, Akhmed introduced the al-Ryadis to Takhmina at the café where he had proposed to her. Anwar and Talgat were not included. Since Takhmina was extraordinarily beautiful, and her small rimless glasses made her look smart and serious, the two brothers fell in love with her on sight. She liked them too, but not so effusively. They were nice Muslim men, she thought, not extraordinary but regular guys. She dropped a few hints about their families, but the hints did not result in any information. This troubled her only a little. So many people were disrupted in these times, and they were obviously very far from Saudi Arabia. The possibility that they might be terrorists did not cross her mind. Terrorists would not be considering marriage or meeting their future sister-in-law. She decided that the simplest explanation for their presence in the Netherlands was the story they presented, that they were here to study and to better themselves. There were many Saudis doing exactly the same thing. In spite of her charm and beauty, Ibrahim remained reserved. Takhmina saw this but decided that she really did not need to win him over. He was only a cousin, after all.

Chapter 32
The Disappearance

One day, Anwar disappeared. He did not come back to the woonboot for dinner in the evening, and when the others looked in his room, they saw that his things were gone. In fact, they never saw him again. He'd flown to the U.S., landing in New York. He told no one that he was going to do this, not even Louise. This was fortunate. She would have been obliged to tell Henderson, who would have alerted the authorities, and Arthur would have been arrested. His absence from the woonboot did not become evident to Charles and Louise for several days, when the other cell members began to comment on it, comments which they overheard, and reported to Henderson. As it was, Arthur had found an apartment in Brattleboro, Vermont, and was already working for a small company that repaired and installed air conditioners when the American authorities tracked him down. He was arrested and held in a jail in Vermont, pending transfer to Guantanamo.

Louise and Charles were informed of his arrest, and Louise, knowing that he would disappear in Guantanamo and likely never be heard from again, flew immediately to Washington. Even before she left, she talked to Henderson, who talked to the President, and when Louise landed she was taken directly to the White House.

Her interview with the President was brief. She explained quickly how Arthur had come to join Al Qaeda and how well he had responded to her therapeutic intervention, and she concluded by suggesting that he be watched but given a chance to show that he'd had a change of heart.

"You make a fine presentation," the President said when she finished and sat down. "Have you ever thought of being a lawyer?"

Louise shook her head. "But when I was a therapist I often had to advocate to my patients on behalf of themselves. Maybe it is similar."

"I'm sure it is, "the President drawled. And he went on. "I'll write a note to Al, the HSO Director, and he'll take care of it from there."

"Thank you Mr. President," said Louise with considerable relief.

The arresting officer grumbled. He had traveled to Vermont to collar the little bastard, which was how he thought of Arthur, and it was the first arrest he'd made in a terrorism case, and they were going to let the guy go. It didn't seem right.

They put an anklet on Arthur, so they would know where he was, and he saw the necessity for it. He went to work every day and began to find his way again. He prayed at a local mosque in Vermont, and he prayed for peace. When the al Qaeda recruiter came around, Arthur was the only one who knew what he was up to, and he made a point of talking to the same young men the recruiter did to let them know that there were other options. He became a passionate advocate of peace and democracy, and he wrote letters to Louise, which she answered using the pseudonym she had used in the Netherlands. She made arrangements so that this correspondence could go on for some time.

Akhmed and his brothers made a lot of money, and found a new apartment in Amsterdam, moving out of the woonboot during the summer. Charles and Louise knew their new address and began to make arrangements to eavesdrop on them, since no one had told them their mission in the Netherlands was over, but before they could do so, the group broke up again with Akhmed leaving for Canada, Ibrahim flying to Istanbul, and

Osama and Muhammad finding a smaller flat in another part of Amsterdam. Charles and Louise lost touch with them. They had given up their cell phones, fearing that Al Qaeda would find them through the numbers, although in fact Al Qaeda had written them off. Charles and Louise could have pursued them through the university records, but they knew they were no longer a threat and said as much to Henderson. The President, having been apprised of the success of their work during his conversation with Louise over Arthur, told Henderson that he might as well tell the two Americans to head for home.

In a year, Takhmina was accepted into the University of Toronto Medical School. She met Akhmed there, and they were married western style. They lived in an apartment in Toronto while she pursued her medical studies and he finished up his university studies before going on for an MBA. They were eventually married in a traditional Muslim wedding, and Akhmed paid a full bride price to her parents in Jordan, after which the parents stopped grumbling. Soon after, the parents came to Canada for a visit.

Ibrahim became, after much further Qur'anic study, a famous Imam in Istanbul, known as Ibrahim al-Saudi, preaching peace and negotiation as the solution to problems. Before he died, he was being regarded by some as a Prophet, but by that time the world had changed considerably.

Chapter 33
The Return

Charles and Louise were wrapping up, putting away equipment and reminiscing about previous assignments.

"Kmedjzik was more scary than fun, I think," Louise said.

"But very satisfying when it was finished," Charles added.

"Hand me that tripod. I'll put it here with the camera equipment," Louise said.

"And the food Larisa's mother made. I'd never had Serbian food before," she added.

"My favorite part of the assignment was the way the women took over the town and created a government," Charles said.

"It was inspiring," Louise added.

"We should write it up and submit it to a women's magazine I think," Charles said. "We have to hide our identities of course and perhaps change the setting or something—to make it more interesting and also to keep the secrets that need to be kept."

"That would be a good task for me," Louise said. "I'd like to do that."

"Can you help me push down this suitcase and get it closed?" she asked.

Charles put both hands on the suitcase and pushed it down. Louise heard the snap.

"That's done it," she said.

"I'm sure we will never forget Larisa," Charles said with some regret in his voice.

"No, probably not. I wonder what she is doing now? "Louise answered.

"We'll have to ask Henderson if he knows anything about her. She'd be almost 10 years old, and I wonder if they could have found a school for her by now. It's a shame that we weren't able to stay in touch with her," Charles said.

"Hmm," Louise hummed noncommittally. Her inclination was to wall off the memories that she was sure would be painful.

***

They finished packing and called the American Embassy in The Hague. They were not surprised to find that Henderson had already alerted the embassy that two very important Americans would be needing some help to fly back to Washington. When they called the embassy their call was passed through to the Ambassador, who greeted them enthusiastically. She didn't know who they were or what they had done to be given such high-level treatment, but she'd learned that some details were necessarily secret, and she didn't have to let her ignorance of them get in the way of her enthusiasm.

"I've sent a car to take you to the airport. 'Two American heroes,' was how the Secretary described you, and that's enough for me."

"Thank you, ma'am," Louise answered. "We appreciate your help."

They went downstairs and said their goodbyes to the café's owner while they sipped their last cup of Dutch coffee and ate some of his famous cookies. Then they took a short walk up and down the street that had become so familiar to them. They stopped and stared for a long time at the woonboot that they'd monitored so persistently. Moving on, they admired the other woonboots too for their fancy curtained windows and colorful paint jobs and the occasional clothes hanging on the line.

When the car came, the café owner helped them get their gear downstairs, puzzled by the extensive technical equipment, but not commenting on it with typical Dutch diplomacy. He was equally surprised by the limousine that came for them, sporting American flags on the front fenders and driven by a uniformed Marine aide-de-camp who loaded their equipment and suitcases into the limo's trunk. Then they were off for a short ride through Amsterdam and out onto the highway leading to Schiphol airport.

The driver gave instructions to a porter who'd been alerted that two *"special"* travelers were arriving. Their gear was loaded onto a motorized cart, and the aide-de-camp escorted them, with their gear trailing behind, to a lounge area, where they were seated in large leather chairs. A waiter approached and asked if they wanted anything from the bar, which they declined. The aide handed them two tickets.

"The next flight to D.C. will board in a half hour. You're in first class of course. Have a pleasant flight."

"Thank you for your help. We are most grateful for all the special attention," Louise said.

"No problem, ma'am," the aide answered before giving a little bow of the head and leaving.

The two American agents looked at each other and started laughing as soon as the aide was out of sight.

"It's a little unsettling," Charles commented.

"It certainly is, after being so inconspicuous for so long."

"Well, we did do a very good job on this case, I think."

"And without any violence," Louise added.

"Right," Charles agreed. "Who was it said "Love is strong as death?"

"I don't know, but we've proved the truth of it in this case."
***

The flight was uneventful, except that the food and service in KLM's first-class section was exceptional. And after a meal, they slept until the flight attendant tapped Charles on the shoulder to tell him that they were on final approach to Dulles and they would have to sit up and fasten their seat belts.

Once the plane had made its connection to the gate, the door opened, and they were the first off. A young woman in military uniform greeted them.

"Good morning sir and madam," she said. "I'm from the White House, and I've been given orders to escort you directly to the West Wing."

"Oh, I see," Louise said in surprise. "How nice."

"Our gear..." Charles began.

"I have made arrangements for all of your gear to be transported directly to an address on Chincoteague Island, VA," she said, showing them a note. "Is this the correct address?"

"Yes, it is," Louise said, after examining the note, and raising her eyebrows when she saw that it was on White House stationery, bearing the Presidential Seal.

"Excellent, she said. "Then, if you will follow me please..."

They followed the woman down a flight of stairs and outside to the tarmac, where a black SUV bearing the Presidential flags was waiting. The driver opened the door for them, and the aide got in the front seat. And in this, almost regal fashion, they left the airport and went to the White House.

Chapter 34
The President

They were waved through several checkpoints. A uniformed aide escorted them into the building through corridors until they were at the door to the Oval Office where, after a brief wait they were ushered in. Henderson was there, as they expected he would be, and they nodded to each other. The President got up from his desk brushed back his chestnut hair and offered his hand. After the handshake he gestured to the couch and all of them sat down.

"Please, sit," the President said.

And they did.

"First, let me say thank you for all the work and extraordinary talents that you have used on behalf of your country."

"There is no need to thank us," Charles said. "We are happy to play our part in the war against terrorism."

"Well, I want to thank you anyway," the President said.

"You're welcome," Louise said.

"I have some news that you will be interested in. You expressed interest after the Serbian episode in communicating with the girl — Larisa was her name, I believe."

"Yes Mr. President?" Louise asked excitedly.

"We have made arrangements for her and her mother to come to the US permanently."

"Oh that's wonderful news!" Charles declared.

"Yes," mirrored Louise. "We'd been hoping that some such arrangement could be made. When can we see them?"

"I'm afraid that will not be possible," said Henderson. "It is too risky."

"But what is the risk?" asked Charles.

"There are some Serbian people in this country–former supporters of Kmedjzic—who might do them harm."

"Oh," said Louise. "I didn't know that."

"I'm afraid it is true," Henderson said. "And some of them are in the DC area. So for now it is best that you maintain some separation from them."

"I see," said Charles. "But how will they live? What will they do?"

"The State Department was very interested in Larisa's intelligence and bravery in putting an end to the Kmedjzik episode. We will help her finish her education and then we are hoping that with some training she can continue to perform some kind of covert support for the US among the Serbian emigres here, who have been recruiting young Serbians to return to Serbia. There may be other missions she could go on also."

"And what about Rosa?" Charles asked.

"We have arranged for her to take English lessons and become a naturalized citizen. We have provided her with a small stipend. They will be quite comfortable, more comfortable than they are used to, I think."

"We are both very pleased with this outcome," Louise said.

Charles nodded vigorously.

"It's the least that a grateful country could do," the President offered.

Henderson, sensing that the interview was over, rose and gestured toward the door. Charles and Louise also stood up, smiled at the President and followed Henderson out the door.

Outside the Oval Office, their sense of formality diminished and they hugged each other in their happiness. Henderson looked on, somewhat embarrassed. He escorted them back to their driver and then waived goodbye as they left the White House grounds.

END

Acknowledgments

My gratitude to the Peace Corps continues, for giving me the time and opportunity to entertain myself by writing this and other works and for the opportunity to learn about other cultures. But The Woonboot takes place in the Netherlands, where I lived some years ago while on a Fulbright Research Fellowship. I didn't have time to write anything then, I was too busy with the research, but I did get to know a reasonable sampling of the Dutch people, and some of their language, landscape and history. So, for this book, I am grateful to the Fulbright Association.

I am also grateful for several readers. First, my talented niece Sarah Starkweather. Second, my team of beta readers — Nancy McBride, Susan Jackson, and particularly Kate Pill, for detailed and accurate commentary and suggestions for improvement. Also, to my fellow chorister and expert in all things Dutch, Bertie Koelewijn.

And I am, as always, thankful beyond words, for my wife Janet Givens, who took time out from her own literary work to help me with aspects of modern publishing that are unrecognizable to this old editor. I continue to be grateful to Janet for just being Janet.

—Woody Starkweather,
January 2018
Deep in the Vermont woods,
watching the winter firs shrug the snow
off their shoulders

About The Author

Woody Starkweather has been a life-long lover of words: spoken, written, or sung. After a long career helping those who struggle with speech, he and his wife Janet Givens joined the Peace Corps and taught English in Central Asia. Now they write– she memoirs, he novels–amid the Vermont woods.

You may contact him at woody.starkweather@gmail.com

www.ingramcontent.com/pod-product-compliance
Lightning Source LLC
Chambersburg PA
CBHW021038130626
46552CB00005B/1906